A Life Less Convenient: Letters to My Ex

Other books by Jennifer Clare Burke:

Visible: A Femmethology, Volume 1

Visible: A Femmethology, Volume 2

Kicked Out, edited by Sassafras Lowrey
with general editor, Jennifer Clare Burke

A Life Less Convenient: Letters to My Ex

By Jennifer Clare Burke

Published in 2013 by
Homofactus Press, L.L.C.
www.homofactuspress.com

Copyright 2006-2013 by Jennifer Clare Burke

Some rights reserved
Printed in the United States of America
ISBN: 978-09855892-0-2

To my father, Henry Burke, who always told me to write, and then to write more. Thank you for teaching me how to keep my *semper fi* alive.

Contents

Introduction

by Jennifer Clare Burke

Homofactus Press has brought *A Life Less Convenient:
Letters to My Ex* back to life in a new form, one that combines
reworked original letters with new letters. The new letters
emerged over the years since the book's creation and release
in 2006.

A Life Less Convenient remains part long–term writing
project and part ongoing psychodynamic therapy. Both
aspects enable me to examine multiple sides of every issue in
each letter as a writer and as a sick person trying to connect
to others. I have learned more than I want to admit about
myself and my exes through using fiction as my lens.

The most striking lesson is one I knew already in my gut:
truth is the most permeable substance out there. Through
this set of eyes, truth is one thing; through another set of eyes
tomorrow, it morphs into nuances with added perceptions
in varying degrees of gray. On yet another day, the truth of
a relationship's ills rings with permanence and invincibility,
only to change into uncertainty later on.

Where conflicting perceptions, multiple interpretations and
unyielding bodily realities collide is the soul of *A Life Less*

Convenient; unfortunately, that's exactly the kind of soul that bumps against the same relationship frustrations, all of which can be told as different stories from different exes. Even within myself, a given story evolves as maturity and experiences color another year of living with disease, another year of loving, trying to love.

After *A Life Less Convenient*'s publication in 2006, I contracted with a new publisher, Homofactus Press, and wrote more letters for the next edition of the book. Homofactus Press assumed an already–published book, one received by readers and worked out in my brain. We talked about the years that elapsed since the original publication and about the ways I have processed disease, love and more in different ways since then.

I am not who I was several years ago.

The new material picks up where *A Life Less Convenient*'s previous publication left off: in the new letters, there is not as much graphic showing and explaining. Instead, there is more exploration of the relational density underlying the envy of a healthy body and more scrutiny of power dynamics against the backdrop of ability/disability. There is more room for loud broadcasting between two people that is never verbalized. There is more room for realizations that happen in connection with a diseased body and occur outside the scope of a relationship, but impact the relationship strongly nonetheless.

Welcome to Homofactus Press' edition of *A Life Less Convenient: Letters to My Ex*. I look forward to hearing from you at *A Life Less Convenient*'s website, ALifeLessConvenient.com.

In sickness and in relative bursts of health,

Jennifer Clare Burke

January 2013, Philadelphia

A letter to my ex about numbers

Dear D.,

Another visit to you brought long stretches of road where I didn't see another car or person. I traveled across states, identifying each one through signs announcing invisible boundaries. I said the names inside my head.

I watched the signs appear for new towns and counties, all telling me "WELCOME," and sometimes giving me numbers that meant nothing: "Home of 1,114." "Population 22,194." I never saw any of these people. They remained as invisible as the lines separating the states.

I expected to see some physical differences after each sign introduced a new place, but the monotony of the land's planes held sway. Throughout seven hours of driving, I kept the same speed, saw the same parade over the guardrail: cloud, hill, rock, cow, field, forest. These marked the way to you.

You chose to live far away from cities and main roads.

I took these trips to you, driving in miles of equal parts silence and garbled radio transmissions, imagining invisible dotted lines carving the earth to match road signs. I wondered if I could find your home on a map, see the streets leading there, gridded out. You accessible on paper.

Instead, you told me about unmarked roads. Your words became the only guide.

I could tell you wanted to be found.

Construction meant delays, but not a total stop. I traveled
at half the speed limit, inhaling dust from a truck farting
up the hill ahead of me. The ride should have been only four
hours, not seven. I kept time, watching the minutes pass on a
cracked digital display near the exposed wires of the Chevy's
damaged steering column.

I grew more edgy as the sun moved lower. As my hours
behind the wheel ticked away, my body assumed its new
habit: becoming leaden, stiff, inexplicable with odd blotches,
pain that revealed nothing of the source.

Time moved. I drove.

Already I knew—without a diagnosis—that soon a chafing
would ignite in my knuckles, stab into my hand, traversing
longitudes to my wrist, elbow, shoulder.

Something new pulsed in me, something wrong. Random
fevers. Infections. Joints that bulged, burning, ugly. These
weren't things I would let you find.

I worried about gripping the wheel with pain I couldn't name.
I worried about coming to you with tight brows, red knuckles.
Cloud, hill, rock, cow, field, forest.

This was not the person I wanted to be with you.

A brown bottle of prescription pills sat on the front seat next
to me. I could have one pill every four hours. Increasingly,
I found myself checking the clock to see if enough time had
elapsed to pop another as pain mapped itself through more
parts of my body. Three hours, forty–five minutes since my
last pill. These numbers meant something to me.

With one hand, I flipped the lid, fished for one sky–blue pill. I
dry–swallowed, let people cut into my lane. Another sign,
another number: "POPULATION: 23,800."

Jennifer Clare Burke

The pill stuck somewhere near my chest, dripping acid rain into my belly for the next four miles. I lost count of everything, except the time it took to reach you and the hours until my next blue pill.

I wondered if I would find a way home to the body I knew before these pills, the body that stayed awake, moving without complaint. I never asked a doctor about this new terrain in my joints and skin.

I told myself everything would go away.

I told myself—and you—lots of things.

A letter to my ex about sunlight

Dear D.,

Neither of us could tell the difference between being shy and being ashamed.

I tried to figure it out. It was one of the few times when I came to your bed during the day. I knew how your bedroom looked in the early morning before sunrise, the barest light faint, forgiving through pulled shades. But the starkness of afternoon summer sunlight left nothing to the imagination.

I first learned what you looked like in the bright sun when we went to your colleague's party. I had already started my beginner cocktail of medications. While I had stabilized a bit, the struggle for health presented itself in my appearance and movements. Look at me once, I seemed healthy, vibrant. Look at me twice and certain angles, a certain paleness, came into sharper relief.

People remained quiet, moving slowly in the exceptional heat that July. We acted no differently from others at the party who lazed at the table. Smoke from the grill occasionally obscured your face. We stayed in the shade under a tent where the sun wouldn't turn my medicated skin into blotches, flares, ugly reactions. We stayed politely at your colleague's place until we left for an early dinner we had planned at your home.

While you drove us to your place, I watched your profile.

Sometimes when you turned to me, I caught more contours of your nose, slight scars on your forehead and cheeks. *So this is your face*, I thought to myself.

"This could be our home," you said, pointing to an odd modern place with unusual sloping angles and a raw wood finish.

"You know where you want to be? You know you want to settle here?"

"Yes, here. It makes sense."

"You already know this is home for you?"

"Mmmhmmm."

At your apartment, we didn't start dinner. We sat on the couch like teenagers in our parents' houses pawing each other. My dress, still on, reached my ankles. I watched the light shift in patterns across the fabric from the sun bouncing through the glass patio doors.

Your shirt came off. Your belt came off. Your neighbors came out. They sat on their deck. You never invested in curtains for the glass expanses in your living room.

You rose from the couch, walking to your bedroom. I heard your fly unzip. I followed.

The bedroom glowed with the sun, shockingly bright. Even with the shades drawn, the sun penetrated, splashing everything in defining light. I could see color variations in the bedspread from washing and wear. I could see old wounds on your back that you never treated, despite being a doctor, how they healed improperly years ago.

So much detail, so visible, everything so bright, even your face, as you stood waiting and happy.

I wanted to slap you because I was awful.

Jennifer Clare Burke

My body was not new to you. No body was new to you, really. Your job involved seeing people in thin paper towels with provocative slits, looking and touching to find a destination: "This is arthritis." "This is parva virus." "This is fibromyalgia." You performed tests, worshipped science, calibrated pathology, talked about clinical trials.

I cursed my luck that I would fall for a rheumatologist, that I would love a medical person at all. Unavoidable. Only medical people surrounded me in those years—at disease lectures, medical conferences, hospital cafeterias, as I went from source to source in different states, trying to find answers. That was how we met.

You were a doctor. I was your favorite chemistry project.

"Well?" You were laughing and joyful.

I stared at my ankles, the only visible part of my legs.

"Look at the sun."

"Huh?" You ignored me, pulled the bedspread back, hopped in.

I started by kicking my sandals off. You watched me now. My fingers undid buttons on my chest. I felt uncomfortable heat in my face.

"Where do you get off turning red?" Still laughing, insistent, but gentle, surprised.

"The sun! It's in this room. All of it."

Your mouth stayed slightly open, ready to reply, but you opted for silence. My dress stayed unbuttoned on my body. This wasn't about you. Not now.

I walked away from the bed to stand in front of a large, wide mirror attached to your dresser. The sun showed everything. I wanted to see my body, to see it as best I could in the way another person would see it.

My dress hit the floor.

There was the sternum, crass, aggressive in the way the skin pulled tightly over it. I turned to the side, seeing how prominently my ribs announced themselves one by one. Needle marks in my ass and arms in various stages of healing glowed in yellow and purple. Red spots burst along my lower spine where the skin had grown thin from steroids, broken in the absence of flesh beneath to provide cushioning.

There was sickness.

I was naked, the Assless Wonder, among other missing parts that had evaporated. I touched my side, fingered the bones. The sharp glare of my collarbones surprised me. As I moved, sunlight caught them like jewelry.

You were sitting on the foot of the bed now, tugging at your ear lobe, a genuinely calm expression on your face.

"You wanted sex before food, right?"

"I wanted to know how you're so sure what's home." I hesitated for a second, then slid into bed. You threw your leg over mine, pulled the covers completely over our heads.

I couldn't see a thing.

"We could go out later to eat, if you don't feel like making anything," you offered.

"Okay, if we feel hungry."

"If? Of course we'll be hungry."

"How do you know?" I insisted.

Some of your hair fell in my mouth.

"Home. Hunger. Whatever. There are some things you know because you feel."

Jennifer Clare Burke

You moved deeper under the covers against me. I heard your breathing change. I stretched fully onto my back, threw my arms over my head, my eyes closed. My left hand slipped out from beneath the bedspread. I felt the inescapable warmth on it. Even as we came closer to dinner, the sun stayed bright.

A letter to my ex about maps

Dear D.,

To tell you the story of my heart, I will tell you two things: my misbegotten theory of the economics of the soul, and the reality of EKGs, cold gooey sensors and booping monitors.

Once, while we sat in the dusty sunlight of your office, I was mesmerized by the way the smell of your unwashed skin, your fabric softener and the newly hung drywall blended into one scent that I identified as "you–ness," even when we toggled through food festivals, concert crowds and dog shit. This moment never left me because of the smell that was you, and because of my idiocy in legislating the heart's economy out loud.

"It should be like the bank, sort of. I'm willing to risk giving you my heart. You can keep it as long as I say I'm depositing it with you, but I should get it back, every piece, when I decide I want it back. I want all of my heart back, every ounce of artery and sinew. I'm not sure whether it has to be in the same shape—I'm not clear on that detail, but you can't keep any of it for yourself after we decide that *this* can't work anymore."

Truthfully, I don't know the shape of the heart. I wouldn't be able to appraise its condition upon return.

I have never known the shape of the heart. In Brownie Scouts during second grade, I slapped together the ceramic offering of an ashtray for neighbors who didn't smoke. I made the ashtray in the shape of a heart, or so I insisted. Its clay folds resembled an unmade bed with tubular formations offering no logic, no opening, no use. The surface appeared to undulate like a living thing.

"This is a heart."

They believed me. Or pretended to. I was happy to give it away.

· · · · · ·

My doctor suggested DHEA to help with lupus symptoms. A good choice, theoretically, supported by enough credible medical literature. I started the drug.

Within days, I was scared by the nonsensical heart thumping, the stabbing chest pain without warning, the baby elephant sitting on my chest. My doctor and I didn't have a relief map of my heart; we couldn't have known what would happen.

It was no one's fault.

At night, I sat shoulder to shoulder with you under the covers, our backs against the headboard, waiting for racehorses beneath my sternum to sleep again. I zoned while watching children's cartoons on television, all the lights out in the room. You indulged me.

I practiced not thinking about my body's misbehavior.

"Maybe it's a muscle spasm in the pectorals or even your shoulders," you said.

"No, this is my heart."

I knew.

I tried to ignore it, tried not to panic at its rate. You lightly traced my chest, collarbones to calm me. I waited, unmoving, for the speeding to burn itself out. I wanted to relax again.

The stress of wondering when the chest pain would return made me tired, snappish.

You brought home my consolation prizes: stuffed cartoon characters, tokens of innocence, of a life without medication consequences. You bought a talking doll that uttered about a dozen inane phrases at oddly auspicious moments.

"I can see your skeleton," it uttered as I held it.

"I'm not sure I like that thing," I said.

"Shake it," you instructed.

I flung the doll up and down. It yelped helplessly. I was happy again.

Things didn't improve during our nights in bed watching mindless television. You rubbed my chest more, hoping the medication would work somehow, despite my heart. I worried about the effects of the DHEA. We both did.

I decided to stop the drug when a giant fist squeezed my heart and lungs without warning. In fear, I literally ran to my doctor, who performed tests immediately. The troponin level in my blood was not entirely cool. My EKG read as slightly abnormal. "Quirky," the doctor said.

A quirky heart.

You could have told him that.

I wore a heart monitor briefly after stopping the drug. People glanced at the white medical tape and cords peeping from my shirt collar. We both absentmindedly played with the octopus–like wires hanging from the sensors at belt level.

The monitor brought good news: my heart was not damaged, the doctor told me, but no more DHEA. I had my whole heart back from DHEA, every ounce, just as I thought I should. My economic theory worked, even if a medication attempt did not.

"Are you okay now?" you asked.

"I think so. My chest feels better. No more pain or racing. There are no lasting effects on the heart's function, from what we know."

"What's the shape of your heart now?"

I lifted my hands to make a shape, didn't know where to place my fingers. Its shape?

Neither of us had a map.

A letter to my ex about bottles

Dear D.,

I found you.

After a long drive, I sat in the car to swallow yet another pill. Hours on the road had passed, miles calibrated by the prescription.

I stared at your address on the mailbox. Your house stood like any other house, nondescript, old. The porch steps needed painting. The gravel driveway sprawled onto the lawn, an uneven mess. Your home.

In the guest room, you put a mat on the floor for me as I requested earlier, calling from the road with swollen, fiery hands.

"But you'll sleep in my room, silly," you said.

"I can be difficult." My voice pixelating into fragments, the connection ended.

I opened the car door, my pill bottle gripped in one hand. You were already beaming at me, leaning over the porch railing.

"You're late."

"Bottlenecks. I was trapped in slow places."

"You're hungry. I'm psychic about these things."

"Not really. I want to lie down for a bit."

"Are you propositioning me?"

"No, no, I wish. I feel like each arm weighs fifty pounds."

"Okay."

You looked disappointed but said nothing as you marched to my car to unload my bags. I wanted to help, but didn't. I said nothing, found my way to the mat, not seeing anything else around me.

· · · · · ·

Consciousness isn't straightforward.

I remembered placing the pill bottle on the floor near my head.

I remembered that the mat smelled like stale rice and the sidewalk outside my childhood home; that the last town I passed was the home of 632 people; that my morning fever was 101.3.

I didn't remember lying down, closing my eyes, the gift of sleep without dreams.

I felt something rustle near my legs. Misty awareness in daylight. Through closed lids, I saw swirling, dark reddish sunbursts as I tried to come to life.

I opened my eyes slowly, woke to you beaming at me again. You sat on a chair next to my mat. I don't know how long you sat there before you grew impatient enough to nudge me out of stillness.

You found me. I rolled on my back, stretching. My hands were stiff, ancient, hard to straighten.

"There you are." Your smile grew by another inch.

"I thought you slept enough." You came toward me from your chair.

I wanted to be just as happy to find you.

But I reached for the pills.

A letter to my ex about fire

Dear D.,

I'm talking to you here, from a place you may never see nor know, engaging in this furtive voyeurism that reveals more of me than you.

While I speak often here of your flesh, you remain immaterial, a hologram conjured through photographs that, like you, don't belong to me now.

Memories of you assume the swaying, distorted sensation of being underwater, a place where sounds are muted so I don't know what was really said. My eyes sting every time I try to see. There is no center of gravity with you. I bob along, treading in a reality that isn't here now.

I remember what became "our" bedroom, "ours" because you bought the furniture with me in mind, based on the kinds of jewelry I wore. I did not suffer delusions about practicalities and realities lightly. I said to buy furniture for yourself that you liked. I told you I wouldn't stay.

You bought the beige duvet anyhow for a bed with a headboard that resembled one of my silver earrings. Nesting rose to the level of art form.

I stopped by to see you, mostly in the dark. You would tell me the day's stories.

"I did laps all around the store today to find sandalwood candles because you said they have the best smell. It took the whole afternoon."

I stared at you, my default reaction when I had no idea what to say. It gave me time to figure out what you were really asking from me.

I labored to decode what you insisted was love. None of this was transparent to me. I didn't dispute that it was love. It was *your* way of loving. I did my best not to begrudge that this was the only way you knew how.

I was missing a script you expected me to know from heart.

Your eyes often said, "Okay, now you! Now you go—your turn!" This was yet another one of those times, so I sat blinking Morse code for "duh." You breathed deeply, went on.

"I looked all around the store because I knew they had to be there, and then I asked three salespeople, and they said noooooooo, no sandalwood candles, there was no such thing, but I kept looking because you said they existed, and I got these three candles."

Pride glowed from your face. I pictured you in a loincloth, dancing in place before a fire, your hand clasping a spear, its point skewering the cellophane wrappers once enclosing the Holy Grail of cheap, scented candles. I imagined your victory dance, the tacky polyester vests of the three salespeople slung over your shoulders like saber–toothed tiger pelts.

You lit the candles, all three. I smirked at the picture in my head. Everything melted.

A letter to my ex about dust

Dear D.,

The first time you offered to do my dishes, I said yes. I sat reading at the table while you washed them by hand. That was our first meal together I had cooked. That was the first time you broke one of my dishes, bits of white jetting in every direction across the kitchen floor.

You looked to me to see how to react.

"Clumsy, you are," I said, not smiling, not frowning. I wanted to see what you would do.

"I am. I fall a lot, too, but I get up, and I'm fine. You don't have to worry."

"I'm not worried at all. But you're still clumsy."

I laughed at you, brought you to bed without cleaning the shards.

That was before my body fell apart, and then we did. There were missed cues, missed connections. These were the months of taking intravenous and oral steroids, learning about bone depletion and resulting bone disease.

I pictured a skeleton of brittle chalk beneath my skin.

We fell apart as the sickie trip set in: there was a tired night here, an aching joint there, always another doctor's appointment.

Then there was the day I didn't board the train with you.

This is what I remember. This is one of the fractures of us.

It's not much, maybe a flash. Perhaps it took fewer than four seconds of our lives. Time has a way of both rushing and slowing events.

We pulled into the parking lot late—my fault. I spaced that morning, half listening to fatigue, half listening to pain, entirely ignoring your urgency to *move, please, now, we have to go.*

The lot bulged with cars belonging to people better behaved than I. They knew to wake on time, not to hit the snooze button, not to eat slowly in micro bites so as not to puke, not to talk to nausea for minutes at a time like it was a two year old needing reassurance.

I wasn't one of these people. You were.

You released the seatbelt with the awkward frenzy of a woman in labor, slamming the door open, tapping the car next to us. I was still seated, taking the keys from the ignition when you appeared outside the driver's side window.

Your feet were already moving away from me.

"The train is pulling in!" you shrieked over your shoulder, already hustling toward it, not missing a step, not missing me.

Molasses seeped along the growing holes in my bones. I held the car door open, stood slowly, surveying the unpredictable bumps and hollows of the black top parking lot, its unforgiving hard surface, the long expanse from the car to the train platform.

You were more than halfway to the train's open door. You stopped quickly and turned to me, feet planted, chest panting.

"What are you doing?" you yelled across the lot.

You took a few steps backward toward the train. The distance was growing already. I never heard your voice sound like that.

I can tell you what I was doing. I was thinking of my knees throbbing, red beneath my pants, even with icing them the night before, how unsteady they would be as I tried to run with you, how hard the fall would be on the ground. I was thinking of how my doctor described problems with bone breaks and the potential ugly flares resulting from the trauma.

Suddenly, seemingly from nowhere, I was also thinking of Mary. And the chalk that fell.

· · · · · ·

In grade school, the nuns handpicked a core of students to be trusted during non–recess hours to take blocky erasers outside, clapping them to the wall and to each other. They trusted that we, the appointed good girls, would not run away from their rosary leashes, that we would return with cleaned erasers and white dust covering our standard–issue kilts.

One day, Mary, another good girl, slipped something in between the erasers. Nobody ever expected a good girl to try a trick, so no one thought to look.

But I looked. I couldn't see what she hid between the bulky erasers until we were safely outside: a new chalk that the nun teaching us seventh–grade English had taken from the supply closet that morning. We started clapping the erasers against the wall.

"Whatcha got there?" I asked Mary, my voice bouncing in between waves of white dust, the last bits of yesterday's handwritten words billowing into our faces.

"Her chalk. I took it. Not the writing kind, but the fat drawing kind for her charts and diagrams and stuff."

She picked up the thick stick of chalk from beneath a fort of erasers near her feet.

"I'm gonna break it," Mary said.

"You're angry at her? Over the last quiz?"

"No. Not angry."

Mary grasped the chalk at the ends with both hands and tried to snap it. Nothing happened, except its grittiness rubbed into her palms. Mary breathed, tried again. Nothing. She stood holding one intact chalk. Her cheeks reddened.

"Are you gonna bring back the broken pieces?" I still had faith in her.

She stayed expressionless and huffed, thinking about the unbroken thing in her hand. We needed to return quickly. We were the good girls.

In turning to reach for another eraser to bang against the school's walls, she stumbled over a crack in the blacktop before catching herself. The chalk flew, shattering a couple of feet away.

A bomb of white splinters covered the black pavement.

Mary drew the toe of her shoe through the white. The dust spread around more, shrapnel creeping onto her shoe. She bent over, fanned her fingers through the exploded bits, trying to shake the chalk into the air. Nothing caught in the light breeze.

The mess grew messier with each attempt to blow it into nothingness.

"They'll see it at dismissal," Mary said.

"Yeah. Accidents happen," I told her, because it was true.

"What accident?"

"The accident where the chalk tripped and fell. I saw it."

Jennifer Clare Burke

Mary finished beating the rest of the erasers savagely together. I did nothing but watch the dust settle on the crown of her head.

"Why did you want it broken?" I asked as we gathered the erasers and headed in.

"Because I can't do this." With her arms full of erasers, she jutted her chin forward, rolling her eyes all over.

"Just *this*," she said, her voice searing with white dust. "I know I can't. It's like I'll be in pieces any second."

We entered the classroom on time, as expected, good girls that we were.

· · · · · ·

I couldn't do *this*.

I pictured myself splayed on the parking lot, bawling in pain, a chalk bomb mess in the places where my hips and vertebrae should have been. I couldn't keep up with you anymore, couldn't take the same journeys that didn't faze you.

"I'm not running." I had to raise my voice to be heard over the distance to you.

"But I have to get on that train! They won't hold it. I have to go to this!" Words as fast as a machine–gun round, your feet moving to the platform. "I can't use the next train!"

"You should go. I can't run with you. Can't do this," I yelled because I needed you to hear me.

Anger, helplessness, sadness on your broken face. These were your only companions that day. I couldn't navigate the terrain. You ran at full speed, your back to me.

My hand had remained on my open car door the entire time. I pulled the door behind me as I landed heavily in the driver's seat. The moment I looked up to see you, the train was already moving, blurred.

Then there was nothing but the tracks.

Jennifer Clare Burke

A letter to my ex about howling

Dear D,

I nearly missed the birthday dinner you planned for me back
then. Time revolved around sleep; sleep revolved around
lupus' timing, lupus' logic. I slept too many hours in a day,
not by choice. Not enough medications lived in my cabinet to
placate disobedient cells.

Prednisone pulses. Provigil, Vivarin, Adderol. I found these
later.

First, I found you.

That was back when you said you liked my makeup and
my confidence in the same grammatically correct sentence,
never realizing the cause/effect connection you inadvertently
identified. You didn't know what you were seeing, but your
learning curve leans steeply. First as my student; later, as
simply mine.

You landed in my classroom, bouncy one minute, reserved
the next. I taught literature and writing. Read this book,
understand this body of work, re–envision the corpus, inscribe
meaning. And revise for a better grade, of course.

I woke each day from long sleeps already waiting for fatigue
to strike. Anyone could read disease on my face back then:
skin looking strange in green, grey and yellow highlights;
navy blue sinking beneath my eyes, made stark by harsh
cheekbones that felt strange when I washed my face.

Disease's face looked odd, caricatured.

I could rewrite with concealing foundation, revise with blush, shadow, gloss. A healthy mirage achieved through force of will and adamant lying. I blurred pink powder with glowing mica chips over my jawline, hid dulled eyes with highlighter pencils.

I told myself it was my social face, something to wear like clothing. I would not look antibody–defeated before a classroom.

I saw my naked face as a series of stories telling the tale of systemic lupus. Eyes with scleritis, retinas with Plaquenil clouding. A mouth with Sjögren's syndrome. A nose with open ulcers in mucous membranes. I kept a supply of cosmetics in my teaching backpack everyday. If I could rewrite the text, then I could edit the disease. Fictions were easy.

My body dragged through the semester. I taught the importance of individual words and multiple narratives in contributing to the whole: learn the history of a single word over continents, carried in a thousand mouths, written through centuries. See a series of prefixes, suffixes, roots, each with a story.

You followed my class rules, submitted work, treading near me in ways I never realized at the time. I began to trust you despite myself, despite roles, with your knack for taking the strange out of strange things, for making them unremarkable, comfortable.

Eventually you moved onto your next semester with more professors and subjects and papers until the sheepskin said your name.

Conquirere. To search, procure, obtain. That was your story, your victory.

Aren't you the precocious one.

· · · · · ·

Jennifer Clare Burke

You find me.

I am no longer your professor. I receive an invitation to your graduation party. Your relatives remind me of everyone and no one, yet you and I are more similar than I would prefer.

You push me more, ask why I taught storytelling as I did, why I chose certain subjects, authors, novels. We discuss the malleability of characters, constructing the self through layers, revealing blind spots in perspective: all essential to fiction and its peek–a–boo truths.

"You're kind of a snob sometimes," you say.

We talk about seeing, its intrinsic ties to desire.

I catch you watching me. I'm off–guard as it happens, then off–kilter afterward when I know, when you come closer.

"Your mascara covers the edges of your lashes and makes them black. But some of the white and gold lashes still peep through," you say, eyeball to eyeball with me, trying to figure out what I hide and accentuate through the same artifice. I feel your breath on my face, punctuation marks of air as you laugh at the discovery.

Once we exist outside the classroom, I teach in ways I don't intend. I teach you familiar clichés—appearance is not reality—and unfamiliar clichés—confidence is not the fatalism that accompanies bare–bone survival as the body betrays itself.

You plan my birthday, something exceptional for that night, only four hours away. You made dinner by yourself and grew a good bit of it in your garden.

How to stay awake, how to be present later? How to fight fatigue when all the day's pills are exhausted?

We linger at the diner in comfortable quiet for bit. Then I say my truth.

"I'm feeling weak. I don't know if this means I should crash before it turns into a bigger flare."

I ask for permission to be this sick. I visualize myself at my bathroom sink with a makeup remover cloth reeking of chemicals: my one step before hitting bed.

Your face folds, crushes in on itself; within moments, a polite expression smooths your features. I think *bed, bed, bed,* watch the redness swell my knuckles, want the absence of connection, of responsibility, of love. Of you.

Air feels watery as I breathe in your attempt to conceal disappointment.

I break quickly to enter the bathroom. Lemons and ammonia mask shit. *Revisere.* I stay long enough to re–blush, re–lipstick, re–powder and beeline to our table.

"It'll be okay. I'll do my best. Call you in a bit before I head to your place?"

A nod from you, relief tinged with wariness. *Now you see me, now you don't.* We've played this peek–a–boo truth before— the one where I don't show up, and not because I have a choice.

· · · · · ·

I've never been to your home before, this one with the farm, the acres, the critters. The rich kid student. I thought I would resent you when I learned at the first student–prof conference about your life, horses, homes. The family money.

And then you had to be precocious.

The map on my passenger seat partially helps. I drive off main roads onto narrow streets through trees and patchwork crops. I hope my coffee kicks in full blast. I will ask for more once I reach you.

After I park in the driveway, I walk in heels through mud, I think. I lean on the front door as I inspect my shoes. Through the screen, I yell, "I'm here. Hi. My feet are covered in horse shit."

"I don't care. Leave the shoes outside and come in," your voice floats to the patio from an upstairs room.

"And how do you always manage to step in shit, seriously?"

I don't—won't—answer that.

Another shout toward the patio. "I mean, can't you just *see* the shit first?"

I toss the heels outside, enter, leave the question unanswered. Three sets of dog eyes appear. Mid–afternoon sunlight illuminates a Saint Bernard and a German shepherd standing in the long hallway. They size me up as a potential playmate, faces inquisitive, benign.

A third pair of eyes looks, but also judges, deciding whether I'm an equal, a threat, a curiosity object to be dismissed. Happy doggy interest is not part of the gaze.

I'm not seeing three dogs. I'm seeing two dogs.

And you own a wolf.

You told me offhandedly before. Sometimes I didn't know when you were joking.

The wolf moves first toward me, leaving the dogs behind. Unable to stay still, unique energy crashing along the wall, the wolf follows its own frequency and intelligence. It craves movement, action. I stay still and observe, an equal participant in the seeing.

A longer muzzle, a longer body than a dog. Sharp, longish face, points and angles accented with contrasting fur coloration. Bodybuilder shoulders atop sleek legs and hips: the contrast should seem off–balance as the wolf wraps her large body around me, circling closely. A rough jostle here and there, which doesn't match the fluidity of the wolf's movement. A coat both smoother and rougher under my hands than a dog's hair. Yellowy–green eyes with intelligence, bright criticism not possessed by domestic critters.

Your footsteps coming downstairs into the hallway. "I see you've met my real family. Stay still. Let her set the pace."

I bend toward her, let her sniff at my face. She licks away makeup. A wolf is not a dog, even when wearing a collar in a farmhouse, even when her breath mingles with mine.

"Alright, it's okay to pet her now. Don't rush her."

Time adjusts to the wolf's timing, the wolf's logic.

She sniffs at my hair, my knees. Another circle around, banging into me. She roughly noses a bruise on the inside of my elbow from a blood test yesterday.

A thought strikes: I might need to be afraid.

I had forgotten to fear a wolf's potential violence.

"Move to her level. Get on the floor." I'm already gone in her fur.

I'm somewhere between kneeling and being on all fours as she moves with me and on me. Her face rubs against mine in short strokes, then longer circles; sometimes her ears bend against the more pronounced bones of my face. I feel the sides of fangs as her lips pull from friction against my skin.

Lipstick, blush, mascara. Gone. Wolf spit, wolf hairs stick to my face and eyelashes. *Conquirere.*

I smell her on me.

The wolf decides to give me a break. With the same edgy energy, she bounds toward the front door, noses it open, heads out. My face feels unfamiliar, revealed.

"She has to be illegal," I remark, standing upright slowly.

"Yes, but whatever. I wanted a wild thing, something real and honest. The neighbors are acres off. She looks like a dog to them when she's in the yard. They can't see the truth, so I don't worry."

"Aren't you scared of her, sometimes? The consequences of what she really is?"

"No." Your face is even, open. "She just is what she is. I wouldn't have her otherwise."

My body heaves from the missed nap. I force myself to hold my shoulders up and back, eyes alert. A broiling wave of razor pain chases my knees and knuckles from their centers outward.

I keep my gaze on you, will myself to be present, to be seen.

You approach, stand eyeball to eyeball again with me, smirking. "Good lord, your makeup is everywhere but where it should be." My hands don't itch to groom and fix.

A pause. No smirking from you. "I like it." Seeing, desire.

"Never saw this before. Your face is kind of a mess with wolf shit all over it. But you're naked too."

The wolf crashes through the now rattling front door. She darts the length of the hall, jogs back, mouth open, teeth shocking. Beautiful, inscrutable. I watch her pacing.

"What she did to you is great."

I forget to feel fearful and ugly around a wild thing I can't control.

A letter to my ex about glitter

Dear D.,

Absolutely nothing was sacred to us.

The gross, the tasteless and the inspired all sat together on a love seat.

"So there you are."

"Yeah, I had a technical difficulty." I looked down at my shoe, giving myself away.

"You walked in dog shit again, didn't you?"

Silence.

"Didn't you?"

"I didn't fall this time."

"Oh, non–slippery dog shit?"

"Yes, it was old. Anyway, I had to clean off my shoes. At least it didn't involve Glitter Turds."

"Do I want to know this?"

"You keep dating someone whose feet are magnetically drawn to poop, so sure you do—why not?"

You were intrigued though you didn't want to be.

"Once upon a time, my parents' dog had a habit of eating anything shiny on the floor, especially any dropped pieces of my mom's crafts for holiday gifts. When my dad did poop duty in the backyard, he noticed turds gleaming with sparkly bits and colors—red, green, silver. Didn't hurt the dog, apparently. Those were the Glitter Turds."

"Heh. I would just leave them as Christmas decorations for the yard. Did you get . . . um, glittery shoes?"

"What do you think?"

"I think you always step in it."

"You said you loved me last night."

"I love you. You step in a lot of shit though."

A letter to my ex about healing

Dear D.,

"I dunno. Something."

That was all I could think to say. You asked, but I didn't know what I wanted.

Something.

We lounged on the third floor of your house. The electricity had been off and on for three days, the result of sporadic thunderstorms and rolling, ongoing blackouts instituted by the electric company. Newscasters reported highs of 103 degrees.

"Is this the fucking desert?" you asked, licking the ice left in your glass.

You wouldn't sit still. You paced, which made you sweat more.

"No, it's way too humid and miserable."

I lifted my thigh off the tiles with a *thwap!* sound where my skin glued itself to the floor. I sat beneath the bay window in your bedroom, holding a vigil for breezes.

It was ten in the morning. We talked about going to the zoo. Then we realized it meant slogging around in the heat, dealing with screaming, tired children and their equally irritable parents. Then we talked about ordering food, but our appetites disappeared with the electricity.

"Then what do you want to do?" you asked, still growly from waking up.

"Um, something."

Annoyed look from you. You grabbed your t–shirt's hem with one hand. It was over your head, on the floor in one move.

"Well?" you asked.

The air felt like water again.

I twisted from my seat on the floor to look out the window. I could smell ozone. All the light was greenish–grey. I knew there would be more rain soon.

"I don't think I want to go out. It's too hot. Plus there's a lighting storm coming soon. Let's just stay here," I said.

"That'll drive me crazy," you huffed. You shook the ice, now small stubs, in your glass.

"I can't go out and move around in this heat. Too many medication problems. I'll be on the ground and dehydrated in no time. You know what that means—an IV, or a doctor visit, or whatever. No," I sighed.

I slapped my hand on a spot beneath the window. "Sit here. Contain your crazy for a minute."

You sighed, trudged over to me, collapsing with exaggeration onto the floor. Sweat–wet hair stuck to your ears, neck, forehead. You looked so young and impatient.

"I've never seen you like this before," I said lightly. Your shoulder brushed mine as we sat beneath the bay window.

You were too hot to lean against me. I could tell.

"Eh, just a mood. I don't know what to do with myself. Maybe peel my skin off."

Your fingertip ran over a sloppy scar along your shoulder as you said "skin," an unconscious gesture.

"What's that from, that scar?"

"Oh, an accident. A wipe–out. That was years ago."

"But the scar is now. Tell me."

"Do you really want to hear this story?" Still growly.

Thunder rumbled like hunger miles off. You rested your head against the window ledge, stared up at the ceiling.

"You're not a morning person, are you?" I asked, reaching to touch the scar.

"See what you get for sleeping over?" You sheepish, slightly.

"Seriously," you said, "we can't stay here. Do you really want to stay in and just stare at each other?"

"Yes, that's just what I want to do."

One trickle of sweat reflected all the light in the room and circled your navel.

It was getting darker. I was getting dizzier, the result of prednisone, Arava, Plaquenil, methotrexate, Flexeril, a recent infusion of Aredia percolating in this humidity. I hadn't eaten right. My head felt like it was floating near the dead ceiling fan. You were not in the mood to be patient.

"No TV, no AC, no nothing," you said.

"We have skin. And scars. We have stories. Let's play a game."

You had never turned down one of my games before.

"I don't know a lot about your body," I said.

"Uh huh."

"No, I don't. I touch it, but I don't know much about it. Like that scar. This is going to be scar show 'n tell."

Wooziness, even while sitting here on the floor. I wondered if you could see it. I leaned my head back until it rested on the ledge. Another whiff of ozone and something rich, earthy. The air moved.

"Okay," you agreed.

You dragged your backside away from the wall to face me and the window. You sat cross–legged, leaned into me, pointing at your shoulder.

"I was biking. There was a metal guardrail along a turn on the highway. I don't know if bikes were allowed on this road, but there I was. I didn't see the gravel, the way it had piled up at this turn. It was like surfing over ball bearings, neat for a while, until I realized that I had no control. There was nothing to hold onto. No anchor. I was skidding on the bike, then I was free, not on the bike anymore, literally flying through the air, until my shoulder went into the guardrail. I had a lot of fragments in it."

"I thought it looked like graffiti, the way it isn't a neat line or a splotch but a combo of both, like it would make a really good shape for a tag," I said.

"What do you think the tag would say," you laughed.

"Ahh, something."

"Uh huh."

The thunder approached. A funny headache emerged over my brows and at the top of my skull, something that accompanied a medication reaction or dehydration. Not a migraine, not a showstopper, but something, enough to close my eyes for a moment, to rock my head once to the left, once to the right.

"Are you okay?" you asked.

"Yeah," I said, the right degree of sarcasm, tiredness permeating my voice. *I am never okay. Not really.*

"Did you forget some of your drugs?"

There was an alertness in your voice. I knew I was growing more listless, pale. That's the way it happened.

"No, I remembered all of them—that's the problem. And now I'm suffering." I smiled as I said it. "It really is okay. It's okay. Tell me about that funny thing on the back of your wrist. It looks like a skin graft," I observed.

"No way, it's my turn. What are those x's on your groin?"

"X's?"

You leaned over, lifted my hips with one hand, pulled my shorts off with the other. I made no effort at all. I wore a bikini underneath my clothes, already anticipating the heat and wetness of the day. You lowered the bottom band a bit.

"Those," you said, pressing the scars between my hipbones.

"Oh," I laughed. "I didn't know those looked like X's, but yeah, they do—you're right. Each one is where an instrument was put in for surgery. That was my second abdominal surgery. It was much easier than being cut from hip to hip, like my first surgery."

I was cooler with my shorts off. You threw them by your side as you stared out the window, rising to your feet. A rushing sound outside, something landing on us through the open window: the first rain that morning, pelting, angry. It was welcome relief.

I turned to lean on the ledge, my right hand thrown out the window. The rain came with such force that each drop stung. We listened to the water hit cars and the tops of window air conditioners with tinny sounds. For three minutes, the outside world turned white with rushing water. Sometimes it sounded like muffled machine guns; at other times, an arrhythmic chorus line.

I did not feel well.

Heat and immunosuppressive cocktails didn't necessarily mix well. I pushed onto my knees so I could put my face out the window. My stomach curled in response; the second I felt it, I placed my forehead flat on the ledge, eyes closed.

A strange fatigue came with the suddenness of the rain. It wasn't tiredness. It was the body and mind deciding to take separate vacations like cheating spouses.

I felt your hand pulling the hair off the back of my neck, releasing it, stroking the vertebrae of my spine individually until my shirt got in the way.

"Lift your arms up," you said.

I barely had them raised when my shirt was off. You tossed it, a perfect landing on my shorts. I folded my arms on the ledge as the rain slowed to steadiness, rested my chin on them, feeling coolness from the rain. Lightning flashed for the first time.

"I wanna do something," you said.

"Something?"

"I promise it'll make you feel better. Stand up."

"Ugh. This already sounds bad."

"No, no, it's what you want. I've watched you do this."

You were already yanking me to my feet with one hand while using the other to push the bay windows all the way open. You maneuvered me to sit on the ledge, facing you, my back to the rain and the world.

"Lean back," you said.

"No! I'll fall. I promise you've never watched me do that."

"You put your face under the sink when you're sick. Or you take a shower. Or a bath. Water makes you feel better no matter what. That's what I've watched. I know."

"Falling out the window will not make me feel better. I'm almost positive."

"But the rain will. You won't fall."

You stood between my bent knees, waiting. Instinctively I wrapped my legs around your waist, ankles crossed behind you, my heels digging into the small of your back. My hands grasped your elbows as you grabbed my hips, thumbs above my X's. I leaned back a bit, testing, enough to get my face wet, but not enough to need to cling to you.

"How's that?"

"Really good," I said.

"Then go."

I looked at the sturdiness of your scar, the grip of your hands.

"Go."

And I did.

I leaned all the way back until I had a full view of the sky, then shut my eyes. Things smelled clean, metallic, earthy, surreal. I lost myself. The rain on my chest and belly was colder than I expected.

Your arms started to shake with exhaustion. I don't know how much time went by when you pulled me inside. You landed on the floor, a wet thud with me tumbling after. My right arm scraped against the ledge as you pulled me in. Rainwater made the blood thin, runny. I looked at it but couldn't tell what shape the scar would take.

You were lying on your back on the floor, panting, eyes closed. I reached for my shirt on the floor, wrapping it around my arm to absorb the blood. I scooted next you, throwing my arm across your chest. Puddles formed on the tile as our hair and remaining clothing dripped together. You finally opened your eyes.

"What's that?" you said, looking at the red blotch emerging through the fabric.

"Something."

My stomach was calm again. The wooziness from the heat and humidity passed with the storm. You pulled my makeshift bandage off, inspected the cut, holding it above your face as we both lay still. It was deeper than I thought.

"I bet that's gonna leave a scar," you said.

I couldn't hear thunder anymore.

"I certainly hope so."

A letter to my ex about morning

Dear D.,

Back when we paced around each other like uneasy, curious boxers, I drove into the city to your apartment.

I knew I didn't want a sudden awkward parting late at night or very early in the morning. I didn't want my body to ruin our night. To avoid it, I stopped at a pharmacy, bought a bottle of pink, viscous stuff for my belly. I gulped it while driving to your home that night.

I threw the bottle on the floor of the passenger side after I emptied it. I couldn't imagine eating that night. I wondered how I would escape a dinner with you. At red lights, I glanced at lipstick smudges on the bottle, now bloody–looking, as if I maimed and drained it alive.

I knew that I didn't feel well quite often, despite not having any diagnosis. I wondered why. Then I stopped myself from wondering why.

I figured the symptoms would go away. People have problems, get better all the time. I grew thinner without effort. My cheekbones became eerily defined.

That night, I told you to cancel the eight o'clock restaurant reservation, to stay inside with me. No dinner for us. You remained hungry, not accustomed to going without. I had learned to numb myself against food deprivation. My hipbones stuck through my skirt like a Roman profile. You bit them through the fabric.

Later you rose from bed and cooked after midnight, half groggy but very hungry. I followed you to the table, nibbling out of politeness—that was my mistake. Afterwards, I returned to bed with you, tried to sleep.

Daggers floated in my stomach. I swore the mattress lurched, but your body was like a statue as your eyes rolled beneath your lids. I watched until nausea took over my body. I eased off the bed to avoid disturbing you, hurried to the kitchen where I put my face beneath the faucet. I couldn't use the bathroom: it was too close to the bedroom.

In mere moments, I heard your voice, ghostly, reverberating self–consciously.

"Did you go?"

I felt water covering my eyelashes as it pulsed from the faucet. I felt light everywhere. I could fly away.

"Oh, there you are."

Your bare belly ebbed over the top of your pants. Your face was lost to me in the darkness of the living room.

"Yeah, I wanted a drink."

Lying was easy.

I didn't want you to know what was wrong. I didn't want you to understand the way my body betrayed me because I myself didn't want to understand.

"Okay," you said, closer now.

I caught the streetlight's gleam in your eyes, on your teeth as you smiled. My mascara dripped. Your fingers stretched over my right shoulder blade to direct me. I could hear our feet on the tiled floor of the kitchen, then on the bare wood of the living room and bedroom.

Jennifer Clare Burke

The nausea grew worse. I didn't know you so well then. I picked up my shirt and jacket.

"I'm going."

"What do you mean? It's 4 a.m. You parked blocks from here."

My shoes on, I started walking.

"Wait, wait, lemme get dressed. I'll go with you."

This was not the last time you helped me fly out your door.

A letter to my ex about marathons

Dear D.,

This is the starvation mindset: you live through a famine once, and forever you horde food and wonder if you'll enjoy another meal tomorrow.

In the living room, I stood in fresh clothes, sweat no longer collecting in sticky pools on my chest and back, hair damp from a shower.

You sat on the edge of your favorite chair. I stood close enough that my legs touched your knees. You reached forward toward me, one of your hands crooked behind my knee while the other stroked my calves.

"You were running earlier," you said.

"Yeah."

"I can feel it. It's still in your muscles."

"It was half an hour ago."

"How do you expect to gain weight if you keep running like that everyday?"

"I have to."

"How's that?" you asked, surprised.

"The thought that I wouldn't use my legs when I actually have them functioning . . . I can't stand it. My legs work now like they used to work before I was sick, so I *have* to use them."

"The wheels aren't gonna fall off the bike just because you park it in the garage for a few days." You smiled.

"How do you know? I've got a walker parked in my garage that says different. You didn't love me back when I was a total gimp."

Your eyes drifted from mine. I didn't know the future. I knew the past. I knew that a perfectly able body could wake one morning with twitching, aching limbs, bobbled and flopped like beached jellyfish.

I knew that love could be tested—and killed—daily through illness and the body's betrayals.

"I really think you would be fine if you lay off running a little. It might even be better for you." Your voice was controlled.

"Better how?" I asked. "Will I be better when I'm crippled again, leaning on four extra legs and having people stare when I try to open a door? Will I think of how I didn't enjoy my legs when they were mine again for a while? There can be another flare."

"That was some time ago. Everything won't fall apart just like that," you said, gentle but insistent.

Your hands migrated from my legs to your lap where they grasped your knees tightly.

"That's *exactly* how everything falls apart."

You sighed, looked at me before gazing down toward my legs. Tiredness appeared without warning in your face.

"You keep thinking that you get to keep your body. That your body stays with you just because you're stuck inside it," I said. "You don't get to keep anything, not really. Nothing's a given."

You sat in silence. I couldn't stop.

"I didn't get rid of my walker for a reason. My legs can leave me again."

Still seated, you suddenly leaned forward, wrapped your arms around my lower back, pulled me between your knees. Your face rested against my belly and hips for a tight moment. I could feel you inhale. Then you let me go so quickly that I needed to step back to gain my balance.

My legs caught me.

You were already standing, your legs moving. You approached the door, hands rooting in pockets, jangling keys. I heard your footsteps echoing on the front porch. Over your shoulder, you yelled to me.

"I'll be back. I need a walk."

I knew just what you meant.

A letter to my ex about nerves

Dear D.,

This letter is about complementary body parts.

This was when my frozen toes fit perfectly between your warm thighs.

By this point, we knew each other better, though your home still remained unfamiliar to me, despite my visits. I walked into closets, whacked my head and shins on furniture.

I shared the reality of my body more honestly with you when I actually understood what I knew of it. I hid less. I didn't need to leave early so that you wouldn't see truths about me.

When we were learning about each other, my neuropathies had not yet powerfully introduced themselves. I didn't know them by name until 2003, when I put my hand into a three–hundred degree pan, felt no pain, wondered how I was burned.

Neurology did not enter my life until I rumbled with what the doctor diagnosed as lupus–induced brain inflammation of the cerebellum. The doctor claimed it hit my startle response, among other things: about every six seconds, I jumped and twitched like someone slammed a door on my tail.

Before that, my neuro system made the occasional odd burp and fart. It more or less behaved itself genteelly.

I simply believed I was preternaturally klutzy. You were charmed.

The early fall created the perfect temperature under the blankets with you. Outside our cocoon, the bedroom draughts gave me chills. I literally ran from the covers to the bathroom for a quick pee.

When I finished, I opened the bathroom door. I didn't know where my foot was at that moment. I heard a longish scraping sound and looked toward the source. The metallic edge along the bottom of the door had swept deeply, completely across my right big toe.

I still have the scar, as real, defined and somewhat faded as these memories of you. I hadn't felt a thing when the edge opened my skin. I was goosebumpy cold. I hopped to the bed.

As I flipped back the covers to swing my legs underneath, I spied the shining dark line of blood dripping across my foot. The door had sliced deeper than I realized. I gasped, half laughing.

"Lookit what I did."

You peered to where I was pointing, the red wetness blossoming further in the minimal light from the hallway.

"Just now? How?"

"I banged the door on it. It doesn't hurt."

"It doesn't?"

You touched my foot, finding that it was, like my hands, icy as usual.

"It's really bleeding still. Are you sure?" you asked, looking at me as you rolled onto your left side, knees slightly pulled up but not fetal.

"Honest. I didn't—don't—feel a thing."

"How is that possible?"

"Don't know. I can tell they're cold though."

"Here," you said. "Come here."

I was stretching on my back when you grabbed both my feet with your right hand, placing them between your thighs above the knees. You pressed your legs together tightly, thighs squeezing my feet.

I could feel some warmth from your body, as much as my nerves would allow. This was the night I bled on your thighs, and neither of us cared.

A letter to my ex about blankets

Dear D.,

"Up?"

Barely a whisper. Someone in my dream is saying it.

"Uuuuuup?"

A groan? A hiss? Something is shifting.

Pressure on the middle of my spine, not unpleasant.

"You wanna get up?"

This is not a dream. Your hands nudge.

I roll to face you. Though my eyes are open, I can't see anything in the room. Darkness undulates thickly, a palpable, living thing.

"No. Wake me in..."

Sleep fits me comfortably, the perfect glove against the conscious world of doctors' billing systems, of smelly clinical latex gloves, of asking for work accommodations.

"In what?"

"An hour?"

I hear slushy footsteps, woolen socks on a newish shag carpet, the slight click of a door shutting. I pull the blankets into cocoon formation, insulation against a symptomatic world.

A blurring of awareness, luscious drowning into sleep.

Tick tock.

· · · · · ·

"You there." The whisper jolts me. Then a comical squeak from—I think—myself.

"It's okay, sorry, sorry, sorry." Someone hugging me.

"Uuuummmmmmmmppppphh."

I move to face you, but quickly reconsider. I can taste morning breath, though it is well beyond morning. I'm waking in the night. My sleep cycle again stands on its head.

I feel wetness from a fresh wave of drool, gooey lines from lip to jaw to blanket. Face–planting in the pillow saves me.

"Umf goooling."

"Everybody drools. I don't care."

I'm pulled into a hug.

"I feel like I'm waking you up for school."

"How long did I sleep?"

"Over nine hours. You sleep in a ball."

"Are you sure? How did nine hours pass? Where am I during this?"

Where does the body hold its hostage?

"I need to shower," I say.

I make a good–faith effort of tossing the covers back, throwing skinny, pale legs over the side of the bed. My feet haven't touched the floor. You turn on two separate lights for inspiration. I have to try.

The day is gone.

The next task is walking. The next task is showering. It gets easier from there.

This is what I tell myself.

· · · · · ·

Coffee and cranberry granola. Caffeine and sweets to reward unremarkable victories. You eat with me. My wet hair leaves uneven, dark spots on my shirt as it moves. I think of my drool drying in the bedroom.

"It sounds so awful, doesn't it? Nine hours. I remember, before all this sickie shit, that I pulled all–nighters because I could, just because it was fun."

I wonder what sleep feels like to you. I've forgotten what it was like when I was a Normal. It was different. That's all I recall.

"When I feel badly about my Coma Sleeps, I remember '98, the year I was diagnosed. On average, I had about four hours of consciousness for every twenty–four hours."

You are genuinely surprised, though a believer.

I'm still eating. I swear the crunch of granola echos in the room, in your absorbing silence. The sound is vulgar, makes me aware of bodily needs always having their way. Since I woke, I feel awkward, as if I've been caught doing something gross, distasteful. It's not that sleep is *wrong* exactly, yet it lacks merit, interest, work ethic.

Sleep is not...*who I am*. I need you to know this, even though you have regularly watched my hours unfurl in bed.

"Around '05, when my health was more stable, I asked my dad about '98. I told him I lacked memories of that time. I explained I had more recent memories. I could list the things I did and how long and how often in '04. I could account for my days. But in '98, there was nothingness. My dad said he had the same experience of me—that I wasn't there. He said I was asleep."

Tick tock. Nine hours of silence spawned a fever to tell in an unconscious mouth.

"There were stretches of time missing from that year, as if I were somewhere else but didn't know it. All I did was sleep. I needed it to control symptoms though I usually didn't get a choice of whether I actually wanted to sleep or not. A body with a fever and that level of illness has to sleep."

These are things you know.

"But mostly, I remember sleep as a way out of pain, a way out of being afraid."

I look down as I speak. I see that I shoved in granola as quickly as I shoved out narrative.

"Wanna go to the grocery store?" Your question is immediate, an intentional laser.

You offer a blanket of chores, the business of living, of placating other—perhaps more acceptable—bodily needs. I nod yes, but I don't shut up, even as you slide my coat on my shoulders.

"It took awhile for the medication and physical therapy to pay off. Then I played with my diet to reduce inflammation. I used exercise to keep my weight up through a lot of lifting. All of that helped with fatigue. I learned to ask for accommodations and to time my medicines to get the most performance out of myself. I always want to look as much like you Normals as possible."

Jennifer Clare Burke

I can't stop myself from telling, retelling. Defending.

I laugh, a flat sound to flatten the truth.

A letter to my ex about horses

Dear D.,

The cold is your cold. You started it.

We barely touch while you sniffle. Yet my cold starts, innocuous until the impact of an immunosuppressive cocktail lands in my heart, lungs.

You heal like anyone else heals after two nasty weeks. My chest sears when I reach the top of a staircase. A little bit of me resents you. I don't breathe well, hit the local emergency room more than once. My doctor puzzles, prescribes.

The following week while traveling, I stay in a hotel without you. When I can't inhale fully, I jump from the oversized bed. I run into a hallway, counting squares on the garish carpeting. I'm looking for air, for the comfort of the herd to hear me if I drown in quicksand lungs. The hallway usually stays empty. No matter. Even if someone is there, I would never say a word. I cough, wheeze, pace, re–enter my room.

"I should have gone to the doctor and fixed it right away," you confess, eyes down, as if there's a cure for the common cold.

Or for us.

"You can't take away the world's dangers to me."

"What if I'm the danger to you?"

"And what if you are?"

I don't heal like you heal.

You panic. I am diagnosed with asthma, something new, and bronchitis, which I choose to disbelieve. When I try yoga stretches, I wheeze face down on the floor, later face down on your chest.

"Be still. Please."

Your body obeys, rigid on the bed, lying on your back, hands thrown above your head. I have you pinned. My fear keeps us both in place. I keep my ear adhered to your chest, even when wheezes and coughs force me to lose contact for seconds at a time.

If I can hear your heart's beat, the rhythm of breaths you take for granted, then I can heal. And I can envy. Resentment and fluid build in tandem, another way we float apart.

There are only so many types of antibiotics, so many times they can be absorbed in mere weeks.

It's not the lupus that gets me. It's the effects of the immunosuppressive treatment. "Immunosuppressive treatment" is Latin for *strange things happen.* Infection causes ugliness, something more than a cold.

Finally I believe.

I call university research and teaching hospitals for specialists in the city. Consultations, screenings, endless questions. Eventually I'm scheduled for a pulmonary doctor and a cardiologist. I wheeze, gag, mark them on the calendar.

The pulmonary doctor examines me, prescribes a breathing test—an hour of frustrating oxygen hunger with bouts of clear breaths. It shows what life has been for weeks. Inhalers, steroids, oxygen in an ambulance. Quick fixes. He consults with the heart doctor before I set foot in the cardiology department. Tests upon tests await me there.

Breathing comes more easily with new medications from
the pulmonary doc. At night, asthma and coughing spasms
control at times, leaving me in a sleepless twilight. Each time,
my hands burrow under the sheets, the fingers of both hands
spread over my sides.

I hold the cage of my ribs holding my heart and lungs. I
wonder if you know what I'm doing. Your chest rises steadily,
deeply in sleep. I lie and wait. In time, I find the rhythm of
my pulse, my breaths, feeling the beats until I don't realize
I'm asleep. But they are there.

· · · · · ·

During World War II, my father slept as the train transported
him and the other Marines from Camp Lejeune to the other
side of the country. During the first night, he woke several
times, thinking he was crazy because pounding hooves from
nearby running horses roused him. He gasped awake with
surprise.

In the morning, he told another Marine about his odd non–
sleeping moments.

"You did hear horses," the soldier told my father.

"There are wild herds of them here, throughout some of the
west. Not so many anymore though. They're used to the train
by now. They even run near it. You left your windows open
last night?"

He had. When he wasn't looking, the world and its wildness
let themselves in, inescapable even in sleep, and always
there.

The next night on the train, he left the windows open,
reassured by the idea of the herd near him. Later came the
sound of free things running, giving into the instinct, finding
rhythm. In the morning, he knew it hadn't been a dream.

Since the nights of trains and running horses, the decades
of his life passed. His life came to the final destination: a

hospital bed going nowhere, lungs eaten by aspirated stomach acid spurted from a fast–moving gastrointestinal cancer.

Sometimes when the drugs kick in with the constant oxygen deprivation, he believes he's at the airport, waiting for his flight, waiting to go. I stop his cancer treatment because he asks me to let him go.

When I give the order, I can't breathe. I bend over, slightly squatting, until I can feel my kneecaps on my forehead. He will die of respiratory failure. Air hunger. I chose his fate.

Cords and lines disconnect from his body. The electronic boops of his respiration disappear with a switch. No more screens of green lines, green numbers, flashing information.

The IV attaches to a port embedded in his chest. That stays. As fast as I can, I have the nurses and doctors facilitate "aggressive comfort measures" that pound through his veins.

And then nothing does.

Death sounds like the steady, barely percussive hum of fluorescent lights.

· · · · · ·

"You'll be getting an IV. Sit here. The tests will begin shortly." The cardiology nurse's clipped, clinical words conflict with her aura of youthful warmth. The pulmonary doctor's office had been much easier going by comparison.

Four patients sit with me. Two have IVs, the cords neatly folded, taped carefully to their arms, out of the way. Two sit waiting. My name rings out, sounds unfamiliar. I follow the nurse. She slips a tourniquet on my arm before my ass hits the chair. The IV is complete before I realize it. I taste salt from the saline flush. She calls the next person's name before I'm on my feet. Assembly line.

Now in the waiting room, three of us sit. We're joined by the fourth, someone with a fresh IV. A small dot of blood adorns the white tape on his arm.

"We'll start the tests now."

The cardiology nurse who originally greeted me now calls names to different rooms. I hit the stress test first; she comes with me.

"My name is Ted."

I smile at her name; she smiles back. Comments are waiting to happen. I'm positive she has heard them all. I won't indulge nervous patter.

I see a syringe of clear liquid in her hand, look at it questioningly.

"I'll inject radioactive material, but not enough to damage you," she explains.

"Radioactive?"

"Yes."

"Will I get super powers?"

"Nope."

"Will I glow?"

"Nope."

I feel pressure at the IV site as I hop on the treadmill. Walking, jogging, running. I'm grateful to move, even if I stay in the same place.

"Next we're doing time–elapsed imaging to watch blood flow."

Ted pushes another syringe of something into my arm. It feels different from the radioactive stuff. Heat steadily courses to my shoulder. We walk to another part of the office, an intimidating setting of too–white machinery barely contained by the room. She directs me to a table in the middle.

"Just lie here. Be still as you can."

"How long is this?"

"Forty–five minutes."

Inwardly I groan.

"Can I read?"

"No. You'll move. We want to see your heart at rest with as little movement as possible."

Once I resign myself to the table, Ted moves the machines' parts around me until they form a cage. She adjusts an empty screen about two feet away to face me.

"We'll need you to be still now. We're starting."

"Should I see anything on this screen?" I ask.

I expect crisp, glowing numbers that change with each breath. I see nothing but blurs in stillness. I strain to focus my eyes, still insistent that something should be clear on the screen.

"No, not yet. It's working though, I promise. You'll see what it is."

I hear Ted touch something, leave, door clicking.

The lights' barely perceptible whirs compete with heaving vibrations from the imaging hulks. Machines working on flesh, flesh working on machines. I can hear air in the vents, the room's respiratory system.

A nurse enters. I remind myself that I can't move to face her.

"Everything okay?" Not Teddy.

"What did you inject me with for this test?"

"It's a type of contrast for the pictures that binds only to the heart muscle but nothing else. Why? Does the IV hurt? You okay?"

"I'm fine. Just wanted to know."

Without a reply, rubber soles slip over the tiles. A door clicks behind her.

I let my eyes roll around the room to pass remaining minutes. I notice the screen is no longer blank. I discern a ghostly, incomplete image of myself: dark brows, pupil, lashes, my hairline, a necklace, my braid resting over my shoulder. These details appear in blackish notes, the rest of me washed out, blending with the screen's border and the room's whiteness.

I replicate my night–time hobby: being quiet enough to hear my heart and lungs function, zeroing in on their pace until I'm asleep. A moment of panic surges when I think of myself as trapped, trapped in my body. But here I can't find my body, can't find myself in the technology mess. The urge to bolt strikes with tingles in my limbs. I will myself to ignore it, refocus on my breathing, my pulse.

Time moves. Data floods the machines. I forget to hear my breath, to feel my pulse. But they are there, animal things that don't need me as much as I need them.

A change flutters on the screen. I don't pay attention immediately, continuing to roam the room visually. My eyes hit the screen again. I see the darker shadows of my features, a more defined outline of my shoulders. The chemical imaging agent—the one that binds only to the heart—is working...

On the screen, I see myself, my alert eyes, my body in drab grays and whites bleeding out to merge with the clinical whites.

Within that dull shell, in shocking layers of brilliant reds, purples, oranges and pinks, the heart runs steadily with me, following its rhythm like a wild animal.

A letter to my ex about stigmata

Dear D.,

"The trees will mock our existence."

"That's slightly horrible to say," you murmur.

You lean back as far as your spine will allow to glimpse the tops of the tallest trees. Other hikers try not to watch you watching the trees. The park, dense with green humidity, occupies a huge chunk of city ground while betraying none of the nearby urban existence.

We move away from the flat main trail with its parking spaces, port–a–potties, water fountains. The side trail is one of many alternate trails, narrower, rougher. Leaves swathe against us like pulses of water, as if we were swimming through trees.

"No, it's good. Timeless. Not horrible. More like...inevitable. They will. They've been here forever. Our lifetimes are just a piece of theirs."

My words hit the air, unintentionally staccato, labored. I'm breathing harder than I should.

We stride uphill on the gravel trail. I pull my shorts away from my legs as everything sticks with sweat. I can feel that my face is a shiny, hot mess, and that I will see bad razor burn on my thighs tomorrow. I'm not deterred.

"My dad and I used to come here. Even when he was into his seventies. He talked about riding horses through this park when he was a kid himself. We guessed at how old these trees might be. He was right: they outlived him and will outlive me. Even you."

The next breath is gaspy, the hint of a shriek. Then another breath, slightly less gaspy, the sound of coming up for air after too long underwater.

"Time—time in a living body—means something else to them."

I eye a flat rock, plop heavily enough to grunt at impact.

You stand over me quietly. "Out of breath?"

Am I?

There are things I forget to monitor. Bodily inconveniences become disregarded muzak.

"No. Yes. Sort of. I mean, my joints are wearing me out. Getting too much pain. Out of time. Sorry."

The sun disappears into sluggish clouds. Humidity quickens dripping sweat between my boobs. Dampened light echoes through trees. A wet smell rises from the forest and from my body—not unpleasant, not perfect, something of leaves, warmth, dirt, fertility, salt, grass.

"We had our hike on this trail. Now we're doing something else." Another inconvenience drown in the forest as if it never happened. Yet evidence of the body remains: puffy red knees, puffy red knuckles.

"Something else" involves a downward trek to the main trail where we parked. The downward trek involves gravel shifting under unstable knees.

There are things I do. Later, in pain, I remember I'm not one of the Normals. You are one of Them.

"Ready?"

I see your eyes on my knees and hands. We both see the flare.

"I hope I'm okay." I speak quietly. I don't want the eternal trees to hear.

"You can outlast this trail. Really."

I push with my hands from the rock, uselessly peel my shirt from my skin. I lead with my right foot onto the gravel...which rolls immediately beneath my weight, which is when I realize the joints in my feet resemble the joints in my hands, my knees.

"I have to do this my way."

I hand over my small backpack. You take it without question as I move downward, putting both hands on the ground. Your eyes widen without a sound as you see my solution.

"I've done it before."

The first few feet of the crab–walk send aches through both hands, both feet. But an ache distributed among four limbs is more tolerable than an ache divided by two.

"Look, I'm not going to have trees mocking me for sprawling ass over head down this trail. I'm minimizing the total damage this way."

With every step, weight lands on my palms. As I feel different configurations of gravel dig through the skin, I shift the points of impact. *This step lands on the outermost part of the palm. This step lands on the thickest part of the thumb. This step lands on the base closest to my wrist.*

I'm slow, cagey, checking that my full weight grounds solidly in the gravel. Each step involves landing four inflamed coordinates on a surface that moves. The last thing I need is gravel sledding on bare, mostly damp skin.

As I crab–walk, my abdomen lays bare, my shirt riding up with movement. My face orients to tree tops, their narrowing trunks, built by centuries for some.

I forget that you're walking near me. Then I see you, with just a few crab–walk lunges left until the main trail.

I try to forget that you're walking.

Once at my destination, I collapse ass first onto the ground of the main trail, a combination of sand, saw dust, some gravel. I look at each hand: a thousand criss–crosses and pocks from every stone's edge, a map of each step to avoid one pain while incurring another, a red pool in the center from satellite cuts.

Your smile congratulates my accomplishment, consoles my defeat. Walking on all fours is both.

"Ahhhhhh, get me up."

I have trained you well: your hands grab at my forearms, not the wrist or hands where joints scream to themselves without encouragement from outside forces.

My knees throb as they balance, bearing my full weight.

"You should see the dents on your butt." Your hands brush pieces of the trail from my backside.

"You should see the holes in my palms." I sound whiny and inwardly cringe.

"Oh, come on, it's not that bad."

You are a person of consistently good intentions, a golden heart, kindness. You are good, too good, with your efforts to make it all go away in a graveyard of inconveniences. I don't bother to think as I shove you, planting my hands flat and fully against your chest. I don't push hard enough for you to lose balance, but enough to reply honestly.

Jennifer Clare Burke

To other hikers, we're a couple in acceptable horseplay, harmless. To you, me and the trees, we're jostling over pain, blood, diseased life spans.

You look at your shirt, feeling wetness immediately. There are two perfect imprints of my hands, the result of your sweat plus everything on my palms: the ground's dampness, mud, grass, and something else - metallic, brutish, coppery.

Within each bloody palm print, a forest of tiny red strokes encompasses the terrain and gathers around the irregular red pond in the center. An awkward stigmata, simultaneous intimations of mortality and everlasting life.

"That was a dumb hipster t–shirt anyhow."

The trees say nothing.

A letter to my ex about steam

Dear D.,

Time shifts again.

My sleep cycle changes through the ugliest of the joint flares. I can't locate waking and sleeping as precisely as I did before. Pain comes in waves, as if someone injects it repeatedly through needles. We count numbers aloud, slowly, through pain's recurring presence as we do when hearing thunderstorms' approach.

I sleep whenever my body says, "Now." Fatigue walks hand in hand with pain.

I am not your playmate anymore. I think you should leave me. My body has betrayed us both.

During the flare, I stay awake through the nights—sometimes—and sleep through the days—sometimes. It's dark at 4:43 in the morning. I'm awake quickly, lying in wetness from one of the monumental drippy sweats that brings me out of sleep.

My breath catches as I feel it in my left leg, something like a razor's burn oozing from my knee up to the hip. Then, other pain: something crushing my ankle from within. I listen to whichever pain screeches the loudest.

You are beside me, on your side, facing me. You hear my teeth snap together. I keep my legs straight, try not to move, as if pain is a predator who might think I'm dead and go away.

Movement, stillness: it doesn't matter. Pain will do what it wants. Earlier that day, I couldn't move my knees and ankles when I tried; the stiffness through the muscles turned me into a cardboard doll.

"What are you feeling?"

You touch the indentation between my ribs where sweat had pooled. Pain sweat smells acidic, leaves usually dark yellow stains on the sheets over time.

"My legs are bad. It's the legs right now."

"What was it earlier?"

"Some one driving wooden pegs with a mallet under my shoulder blades, and every lymph node in my throat and armpits in revolt."

"Wanna wrap them?"

"Yeah. Might as well."

You reach for the series of neatly bundled cloth bandages that I keep on the nightstand across from my side of the bed. I alternate between wrapping and stabilizing the joints as they turn red, tantrumming from a malfunctioning immune system, and leaving the bandages off. The bandages are a requirement if I need to go out and walk. During some of the flare, I turn into the invisible woman: I stay in. No one sees me if I can help it.

You hand me two bandages, one for each knee. You watch quietly, your hip next to mine as we sit on the edge of the bed. On automatic pilot, I mummify each knee. Without saying anything, I amble to the kitchen. You follow.

Like a choreographed routine, I reach for bread; you heat water. I grab the toaster, stuff in bread while you stir instant coffee. We know how to move around each other.

My face feels puffier than my knees. Larger steroid doses than my usual daily dose make my cheeks and jaw swell until my head feels like a mushroomy flesh under my fingers. I turn off the overhead light, switch on the small oven light. Still dark outside. You smirk. You know what this is about.

"I *know* how you look."

"See, that's one of my problems. I feel ugly enough from pain and not being able to do anything, and then the treatment makes me hideous. And on top of it all, I'm a hairy beast."

"What, your legs, you mean?"

"Among other things, yes—they're the worst offenders. They're offending me in every way, actually."

I pull the gel ice packs from the freezer, sling them over my arm as I grab the toast, move into the living room. I sit on the floor, my legs splayed out like a doll without joints straight in front of me as I lean against the couch.

One ice pack over each knee. I gnaw the crusts off the toast first. You land on the couch behind me, your knee bumping into my shoulder, your hand on the remote.

"Let's watch something totally stupid," I say.

I hear the clicking of the remote, but I don't look up for a while. I watch my knees, as if I can play sentinel to the pain, map its course, cut off its supplies as it treks across my joints.

I flip the ice packs off my knees, roll onto my side, push my hands against the seat of the couch to stand up. I can't rely on my knees and ankles to be there for me. I don't blame them. They huddle under assault. I stagger and trudge to the freezer to put the packs back. I look like a stoned ballerina who doesn't know she has a bad case of drop foot.

More alternating: time for heat, bandages off. I head toward the bathroom for a hot shower.

"I'll go in late today," you say. "I have a very flexible boss."

You are your own boss. You own the place.

"Why? I'm fine on my own here."

"Wanna shave?"

"What do you mean? No. I can't bend my legs, and at this rate, I wouldn't trust my hands because the knuckles are so shitty with this flare. Wait, why are you going in late?"

"Because you'll be in the bath, and I'll shave your legs."

I envision hordes of toilet paper nodules decorating both legs like frozen confetti.

"Have you ever shaved anyone else?"

Pause. "No." You look a little defeated.

"My knees and ankles are very knobby."

"They're like everybody else's."

Exasperation, slight, an undercurrent, but there. You are trying to do something nice, and I'm scared of being hurt, of more pain.

"What's worse—hating your hairy legs or getting a nick here and there?" you ask.

"You already plan on nicking me?"

I'm being a jerk, and I know it. I don't know why. Since when did shaving become a power contest that was so intimate? Since I realized that a basic bodily function had to be entrusted to someone else, someone more able–bodied than I, because I couldn't pull it off while flaring. I turn on the faucet, letting the tub fill.

"How do you want to do this?" I ask.

I put my hand against the tiled wall, lift my right foot off the floor. It's like someone shoving a hypodermic into the deepest part of the joint and using the needle like a car jack. I blow air out forcefully.

"Teeeeeeen, niiiiiiiiine, eight, seven, six..."

You're quiet when my eyes open and meet yours.

"Will you get in with me?"

"Nah. You get in the tub and soak, and I'll sit out here on the floor, leaning in."

"Okay."

I sit on the toilet as I undress. Once my clothes are off and the tub is full, you grab me by both biceps to lift me. I can't use my legs to push off the seat. I take a few steps to the tub. When it's time to hop in, you grab me around my sides.

"This feels like a bird's rib cage."

There is no muscle, no flesh. It burned off with pain, medications, the lack of activity. Some sound, somewhere from behind my lungs, eases out of my throat as my body submerges. Heat. Floating. Then you with a razor. My elbows are being stabbed by something hot, slicing. My teeth snap shut to handle it. For a few seconds, I don't breathe.

You lean into the tub, one hand lifting the arch of my foot, resting it on your arm. The other hand rubs water and lathered soap on the front of my shin.

I wonder how my face looks to you. You're concentrating, the first bits of fear appear across your eyes as you look back. Maybe you are mirroring me.

You shake your hand in the water to rinse it and pick up the razor on the edge of the tub. The first touch of the blade, you pressing to get the right gauge on the pressure, then gliding from my ankle to my knee. No blood. No casualties, except our doubt.

You shake the razor in the water, return it to the ledge. Your hand twists the soap, gets lather, moves over the next inch of flesh. Another swipe with the razor, slow and plodding, careful.

We don't say anything, afraid to disrupt the bloodless spell. I feel strange and revealed every time I catch your eyes, so I stop looking at you. I watch the blade and my skin.

It takes forty minutes to do both legs from the top of the ankle to just over my knee. That's plenty. The task is making you tired from the awkward angle and the level of concentration. I'm happy.

I'm also covered in foamy water flecked with black, short fur. I grab the support bar in the tub to pull myself up. The aching abated in the hot water. I feel slimed from the shaving grime.

"Oh, my back's stiff," you say, rising slowly.

"Then let's both get in the shower to rinse off."

You don't need another invitation. Your clothes are off quickly as the tub drains the last of the bath water. You turn on the shower and step in. I give you the full spray, watching it bounce off your hair and shoulders as you roll your head around.

"Now you," you say.

We switch places. Wisps of steam rise from your arms. We both like water hot enough to burn. It hits my neck and belly.

"What if I'm never okay?"

"I can't answer that. Move over, and we'll share."

Your chest bumping into me, more steam, a sense of lightness from the heat and rhythm of the water.

"Did I do good?" you ask.

"Perfect, really."

Jennifer Clare Burke

"Did you think I would hurt you?"

"Yes," I say, because the worst is over, for now.

I can't hear what you say next. Your face is under the water as you speak. I can make out two syllables but not the words. I guess that you're asking me, "How come?"

I reply, "Well, I thought you'd hurt me because it just happens. You try to help someone, and you hurt the person instead. That's the way it goes."

The shower loses some pressure. I know our time is almost up. You turn around to me, eyes red from being directly in the stream.

Face to face now, I say, "That's what you asked me, right— why I thought you would hurt me? Is that what you asked?"

"No, I didn't ask that," you respond quietly, almost smiling.

Water pools in your collarbones before channeling down.

"Then what did you say just now when you were turned away from me?" I ask.

"I said, 'Me too.' I also thought I would hurt you."

You shake your hair like a dog before shutting off the water. You reach for my hair, hanging in one thickened wet rope over my chest, twist the water from it. We watch it slosh down my thighs as you squeeze. When my hair is wrung out, the remaining drops feel lighter than feathers.

"We both thought I would get hurt, and we both did it anyhow," I say to myself more than you, my eyes closing as another wave hits. I feel pins burrowing into my knuckles. My left knee won't straighten again.

"Of course," you say. You aren't smiling.

Under my hands, your face is delicate.

A letter to my ex about limits

Dear D.,

The wall still has marks, fingernail–like etches that penetrate
multiple paint layers and the plaster. It's hard to believe
I possessed the strength to mark a wall like that. Can ten
swollen joints run the errands, clean up and get to work on
time? Can a low–grade fever and a migraine work extra hours
to afford the medicines not covered by insurance?

Yes, all that and dent the wall.

Anger morphed into lava, a viscous thing with a path in mind;
lava wants escape, a place to go, or at least wind up. The
lamp was small, nearby, fit well in my hand.

You saw the future, standing behind me as I picked a target,
your voice weak, thin: "Just don't hit the computer. Your
writing is on it."

The force of my throw, the kickback in the muscles of my arm.
Then the sound exploding against the wall, against us. Ever
since the onset of disease, the world, even myself: they all
come at me ass–backward.

A small piece of plastic embeds in the wall at the base of one
plaster rivulet.

There is the lamp and its shape. Then there is the impression
any given item makes when it is thrown, when it breaks.

Minus one lamp, we trudged on, a choice together, a commit–ment. We learned the value of delegating chores, of managing hurts when they happen, of adequate rest, of finding time not to think, but to be.

Aspirations are fine things, made of the same ether surrounding Mount Olympus. If gods could fuck it all up, how did we expect to hang in there?

. . . . . .

Morning, or something like it. Now is not dawn or sometime shortly after. Afternoon light in early winter seeps through the room, syrupy and encompassing.

Mid–afternoon is my morning. I rest until I'm ready to move. Today I'm allowed such indulgence: work a few days, push extra hours with pills designed for that purpose, then collapse until the cycle is repeated.

There are the basics of life awaiting me: teeth needing a brush; body needing a shower; belly needing food; a home needing me. I contemplate the to–do list. Without a conscious decision, I sleep for another hour. When my eyes open, the darkness is complete. Night. My body screams for its meds.

A thickness in the brain and in the limbs refuses to dissipate. Part increased Flexeril from the night before, part reality of a body simply saying no. Minimal effort today, except for calling up the strength of Hercules to push through the leaden fog.

Today the lower body takes the worst of this hit. Movement from bed means movement of hips, knees, ankles. I work with each joint, each side, to navigate stiffness and gravity. The too–cool air coming from the window—left only a half–inch open—increases the spasms. I work my way to the offender, manage a satisfying slam shut. My arms are somewhat happy to be alive today, even if my neck protests.

I hit the underwear drawer, then pull thrown clothes from the back of the bedroom rocking chair. I realize I forgot to do laundry. Instead, I acknowledged laundry, found the chore impossible on top of work, physical therapy, work, a hospital visit for a doctor's appointment/injection/labs, work, family needs, cooking....

Got lamp?

Not yet. I have options before furniture meets wall in a head–on collision.

I pull on yoga pants slowly, first standing, which I abandon, then sitting, lest I tempt fate. Stress, fixating on the next thing to be accomplished along side the next pain to be managed. There are options, I remind myself.

"Option" becomes a verb in this scenario: it's the act of making choices creatively around "real life" and disease. On good days, I can. On bad days, I know the emergency room staff's first names, inappropriate details about their families, politics, bodily habits.

I search for my shirt, find it, put in on backwards, try again. When I open my sock drawer, I find no socks.

Perspective: this is not a tragedy.

Because it's not.

I tell myself again.

My hips groan as I remain leaning forward, staring at the drawer, willing clean socks to materialize. Later, I will bend a spoon.

I already hear your voice floating in my head. "It will be okay." Knee–jerk optimism: it saves you every time, keeps you close to me. I do not tend toward the half–full glass. I visualize ways for the glass to shatter under pressure.

Options. Lamp. Options. Lamp.

I grab my winter coat, my flip–flops. As fast as my body allows, I hustle to the apartment building next to mine for the basement laundromat. I remind myself that creativity takes all forms, including the gross; that aspirations become lived experiences through conscious perseverance; that Hera and Zeus probably divinely repelled dirt and body odor and didn't have these problems; and, most importantly, that my feet are cold.

The flip–flops' slapping on the linoleum floor echoes as I approach the Lost 'n Found basket. A frazzled woman with long, unkempt hair, rummaging in a laundry basket in a winter coat, long pants, flip–flops: I am not inconspicuous.

I'm alone with the basket. Grateful for both. My hands don't want to touch other people's clothing, linens, lives.

I find a large pair of heavy tube socks. I make a point of not scanning the room before I head to my apartment, where I cut the socks at the ankle, turn them inside out, pull them on as my brain releases an "ew" that's quickly replaced by "ah." Socks. Warm socks.

My socks? Yes, now.

Clean socks?

Life among mortal failings is rarely ideal.

Later that day, prednisone, Provigil and caffeine work their magic. I tackle the chores, prioritizing laundry above grocery shopping, cooking, shaking rugs.

When you come home, your eyes catch a ramble of jagged threads peeking over my sneakers.

"How did they get like that? Never saw those before."

"They're new. New to me."

Puzzlement.

"I had no clean laundry, no socks, nothing. The stuff in that Lost 'n Found basket has been there forever, so I helped myself."

"You didn't wash them first? You don't know where they've been!"

"I know where my body has been this past week, and it wasn't doing laundry."

"Ugghhh, that's awful. You just took them?"

Silence. A few beats.

"Cold weather, cold feet, no socks."

"Just wear your own dirty socks."

"Lord no. Those are truly awful. I'd rather take the gamble that these socks were washed and left behind instead of the certainty of my own filth in the hamper. If I had more hours in a day of being awake and pain–free enough, I wouldn't have this predicament."

The smile starts. "That's...true." The giggles. "I can't believe the stuff you'll do."

"I'm impressed with my problem–solving."

You head to the shower while I retreat to my computer. Hours later in the bedroom, the tv is a flickering hearth selling us something every seven minutes.

You turn on your side to reach the lamp, your sign that it's time for sleep.

"I have learned something about you today," you say, your eyes heavy.

I'm surprisingly drowsy, given the uppers that must be still pulsing in my blood.

I hear the lamp's click.

A letter to my ex about magic

Dear D.,

I didn't know when it opened, a portal to shame and the truth about subtle disintegration.

Less than the size of a dime, a hole burrowed into the flesh covering one pronounced vertebrae in my lower back. Maybe it first opened with a passing twinge, something I had rationalized away with everything else that meant my body didn't know itself anymore. You didn't notice at first. I was a magician and made things disappear.

After the diagnosis and the full–throttle onset of disease, I dropped below ninety pounds. Thinning bones ground into thinned flesh. My skin lost its elasticity once my steroids increased. Flesh, like bone, broke down more easily without much pressure. Skin became another new something to lose.

I threw myself into contortions to see the hole in the mirror after I locked the bathroom door. I needed to check and recheck the way my skin decided to pull a vanishing act. The exposed flesh gleamed red, wet–looking. The surrounding skin morphed into a swollen, hostile, pink aureole.

The portal didn't heal quickly or easily like a cut. The hole wasn't injury; it was deterioration.

I adjusted.

I changed my habits. I shifted the way I sat in chairs. I no longer slept on my back. I bought more bandages. I watched where your eyes went when I was undressed.

You sat in bed before sleeping, leaning against the headboard while reading, as usual. I performed my habits too, throwing my bra on the chair near the closet. I slid my jeans over my bare feet, realizing that I had just commanded your full attention.

"You almost finished reading?" I asked.

"I can be finished now."

"No rush."

I headed to the bathroom, where I undressed completely. When I returned to the bedroom, I reached around the doorway, snapped the light off before you could see me. While I pulled the covers down, I heard you place your book on the table next to the bed. I eased onto my hip, never letting my back take the brunt of my weight as I landed, and stayed on my side.

I pulled the covers up to my shoulder, rested my head on your chest. You never realized the sleight of skin.

This bathroom routine for changing worked until you tried to undress me one night. By the time you reached my belt, I grabbed your hand.

"What?"

"I wanna brush my teeth."

"Right now?"

"Yes."

"Then let me finish this first."

You licked my neck, pulled at the belt buckle. I pulled away. I took off the rest of my clothes in the bathroom and brushed my teeth, just to be honest.

I was staring down at the laundry in my hands when I walked back to the bedroom, where you stood in the doorway. I couldn't reach for the light switch. My old trick couldn't work now. I took a step backward.

"What?"

"You surprised me, that's all."

Lying was easy.

"Come here." You stepped back into the room as your hand sealed around my wrist. You were inches from the bed, and I had to think of something.

"Lie down, I'll rub your back."

Abracadabra.

"Okay," you said, turning quickly to lie on your stomach in bed, your attention away from my body, focused on your own.

I left the light on, massaging your back. Your muscles twitched as you fell asleep.

For a while, I hoped the portal would close, become normal, that flesh would return to stay intact. Over the next weeks, the hole reached various stages of healing and closure, only to open anew, leaving runny, blood–brown imprints on my clothes.

I waved a wand, pulled rabbits out of a hat. I found ways for you never to see my back undressed in the light. I couldn't form a decent scab to save my dignity.

It was in the dark and closeness, in touch, that you found the portal.

I was lying on top of you, staring nose to nose as we talked, your hands grazing my back. I lost my vigilance, kept babbling, didn't detect your ginger fingertips circling the wound, which had grown rough and scaled around the edges. I tensed the moment I knew what you were doing.

"What?"

"You're touching something new," I explained, hesitant. It wasn't new. I had been hiding it in one way or another for weeks. It was new to you.

"A callus?"

I didn't want to show you another way my body found to betray us.

"Sort of."

"What?"

"It's like a cut, but it keeps opening. I don't know how to heal it. It's right on that bone."

I felt anger out of nowhere.

"Will the skin come back?" you asked, concerned.

I didn't know. I had cared for the wound since it first opened. Healing no longer took a direct course: the portal closed slightly, scabbed over, promptly bled again when I least expected it.

"I don't know. My skin didn't come with a return policy."

A letter to my ex about peanut butter

Dear D.,

The body is the site of sickness as well as love. That's where things became messy in our world.

The clichés are the hardest to overcome in love. Eternally cheesy, clichés hold all the truths (this very sentence is one). Here's another: being loved is far harder to accept than loving another.

You knew I was sick from the beginning. You listened to all the words I used to describe a day. Ache, needle, stiffness, hospital, fever, hours.

You struggled with, but accepted, many things about me. I wouldn't cut my hair. I insisted on wearing dangerous shoes. I could share a bed. I wouldn't share my hospital room.

"You were at the hospital?" you asked, incredulous, early in our relationship.

"Yeah, a few hours in the ER, but I was out this time without any three–day layovers. I couldn't get the puking under control on my own." I shrugged.

"But you didn't call me. You have to call me," you insisted.

"And why would I do that?"

You stared at me.

"Who wants illness?" I asked.

"It's because I want you that I would go when you're in the hospital, even if it means wiping peanut butter from your lips."

A letter to my ex about gifts

Dear D.,

We left the party for your business partner, the party I never wanted to attend, but did. We came home early, wilted from the late August heat, flopped together on the battered sofa.

We sat silent as you rubbed my back for a while. I felt the width of your palms on my back. I lost track of time. I was still in my dress, my hair loose and, by that point, messy. I turned toward you, leaned into your chest, then stretched fully across your lap. Your hands moved into my hair.

"We have to wash the car."

"You mean we have to wash your car," I said.

"Well, yes."

"It's okay. I'll do it. I said I would."

I felt your fingers take one chunk of my hair, twirl it into a coil, then shake it loose, pulling it straight again. I didn't move. I thought about it, though.

"I don't get to see or touch your hair," you said. "This is rare."

"It *is* rare."

"How come I'm allowed to do it today?"

"Because I'm too hot and sleepy to stop you. And it's not like you're not allowed to touch it other times."

"Yeah, but you never let it happen other times. There's no chance. Like it's untouchable."

I felt my lips tighten.

"Are we washing your car or not?"

"Yeah."

"I should get changed then."

"Can you leave your hair down?"

I eased off your lap, gently. I didn't know if I could leave my hair loose for you. I changed in the bedroom, leaving my dress in a wrinkled heap on the floor. Instead of braiding my hair or pulling it upward, I tied it in a loose ponytail, a compromise.

Access to hair. You didn't mean to ask for the impossible.

I was no Samson. I knew that for a fact. I had already lost my hair, then gained strength when it happened, but not without enduring the crushing disorientation.

You didn't know what was lost to me back then. You couldn't know, not now, not after playing with over two feet of hair locked securely in my scalp. You didn't know what was in my closet. Literally.

On the floor toward the back, a spherical, silver pot lined with plastic sat in dust bunnies. It contained the hair that fell out of my head in 1998.

When lupus and other shades of illness first hit, I didn't know what would be destroyed. When I went to my rheumatology appointment, I was diagnosed with systemic lupus and Sjögren's syndrome. The doctor provided a pamphlet on kidney failure and transplants, ordered an echocardiogram for the lining of my heart, and categorized by numbers the loss of mobility and pain in each joint.

My brain held images of tornados passing through towns, shredding one house, leaving the one next door intact. No one knew what would be saved or destroyed completely. I watched the illness and drugs pass through my body, wondering what would be left whole afterwards.

At first, I ignored the hair congregating on the brush, the bathroom floor, the pillow and blankets. I ignored that a good tug would land so many strands in my hand. I talked to my doctor about my new habit of ignoring my hair, specifically the hair that was not in my head anymore.

"Hair loss is one of the symptoms of lupus. It could also be your body adjusting to the drugs. And the stress of dealing with all the changes. Let's keep track of it and your other symptoms. Could be just another symptom. Everyone's lupus is different; people get different combinations of symptoms."

It was not another symptom.

It was my hair.

Thin spots the size of dimes emerged; by then, I was already defiant. I did not accept loss graciously.

· · · · · ·

D., there are things I don't expect you to understand.

There are things I want you to know. I don't want to be afraid anymore of whether you know. If I give them to you, then no one can take them away from me.

This is what I did.

I became the hair cop. I went to the scenes of the crime to inspect the victims. When I saw strands abandoned on my pillow in the morning, I gathered them. When my brush grew clogged with hair, I pulled out the thick web between the bristles. When I saw what covered the bathroom floor after a shower, I scooped that hair, too.

It was my hair. It needed to stay my hair, even if it no longer stayed on my head. What fell out was not trash. It was me. I wasn't going to have my hair taken away. I found a way to keep it, which eventually raised logistical issues. At first, I kept the beginnings of loss in a shallow plastic container with a resealable lid.

In time, the container wasn't big enough. I had more of my lost hair to keep in a container, or rather, more of the self that no longer remained part of me. The hair was still mine, all the length of it, all the inches I refused to cut even as it fell out.

When I picked the hair up from any surface, I started to twist and knot it, as if my hands instinctively knew that long hair should be pulled up into a twist or a braid, no matter where it was found.

I deposited knotted balls of hair like yarn into the large silver pot once I realized the smaller container couldn't handle the ongoing debris from the tornado.

Those were days of strange rituals.

Later, I showed you different hair rituals, like obsessively braiding my hair or pulling it up out of reach, any style that was tight enough to bind my hair to me so that nothing could take it away again.

My body was more stable by the time you loved me, but my mind was not. My mind stayed in starvation mode.

"Can you leave your hair down?"

I did leave it down. It's down. It's still on the floor. It's still mine. I own it. It's in my pot if not my scalp.

I didn't say that.

Instead I went outside to the driveway where you had your car already wet and soaped.

"A ponytail! Look at you."

"It's kind of loose. Be happy."

The sun hit the trunk, while your home kept the car's front shaded. You handed a bucket of soapy water and a sponge to me, then returned to your spot in the sun, scrubbing the rear bumper.

Outside for a only few seconds, I began sweating in the heat. I got to work, my ponytail flopping around my neck, sticking then re–sticking to my skin. I wiped sweat from my forehead into my hair, using it like a cloth. I had forgotten hair had uses besides being a caged, prized animal.

Your clothes grew transparent with sweat.

Once the car was scrubbed, you took my bucket and yours to dump the dirty water. I stood, waiting, fingering the wet tendrils of hair that found their way into knots on their own. When you returned, you plunked both buckets of fresh water near the car.

Then your body folded onto the grass a couple of feet away, your face red, strained. You sat, throwing your head forward on bent knees. I thought about rushing toward you. I didn't move. After a deep breath, you leaned back, your hands supporting your weight, head upright.

"I think the heat is getting the better of me," you said.

"You're the one who got stuck in the sun, not me. Will you be okay?"

"Yeah, I just gotta stay still for a bit."

"That won't get you cool, though."

"Eh."

You pulled your soaked shirt off, threw it in the grass after wiping your face. I reached for the band holding my ponytail, inadvertently flicking sweat beads from my hair as I pulled, letting the band fall on the ground. For once, I didn't check the band for clumps of hair that hadn't fallen out in a long time. I swung my hair loose, walked to the buckets of fresh water, leaned over one, lowering my head slowly into the wet.

The sharp coolness on my scalp was an unexpected relief. I reached through my hair to submerge each strand completely. As soon as I began to straighten, I could feel the weight of my hair, dense with re–grown mass and water. I walked toward you, slightly crooked, supporting my hair with one hand as cool rivulets trailed toward my elbow. You started to move once I came next to you, droplets already falling on you.

"No, don't move. Just stay here."

I didn't see your expression. I never took time to look. The water dripped quickly. I didn't want to waste it. I walked behind you, turned to stand with my back to you. I lowered myself carefully, my back sliding against yours until my butt hit the ground.

"Here."

I flipped my hair back, listening to it whip over your face, shoulders, chest, wherever it could reach you. A flesh–slapping sound as my hair landed, then you sighing, moving into a groan.

Minutes passed. After I pulled my hair from you, I stood up, walked around to face you. I grabbed your hand, pulled you to your feet as water still dripped from your face, making you blink.

I scoured your skin from your scalp to your belt. No dearly departed strands. Confusion and amusement spread across your face.

"What are you looking for?"

I ran my hands over your neck, chest, arms for one last check. None of my hair lost.

"You."

A letter to my ex about seams

Dear D.,

We took on my second abdominal surgery together, sort of. Together, to the extent I let you near me.

We decided to cut the stitches because they became thorns to me, bitty spurs poking my skin, catching on clothing. They grew hard and brittle. I scheduled an appointment for the surgeon to remove any stitches not yet dissolved. But while waiting I grew restless, uncomfortable.

Neither of us had ever removed stitches. A few things motivated me—and then us—to consider removing them ourselves. The surgeon's appointment would cost ninety dollars or more out of pocket for quick snips. Then there was curiosity, even the sense of conquering, to see if we could cut the stitches without problems.

The stitches looked dry, if a little scabby, free from redness. The swollen pooch of my belly receded. I felt more energy. I was healing.

I wondered how we should do it—where to sit or stand, what to use. Your avocational carpentry skills came in handy: your eye for angles, positioning, tools; your intuitive ability to put things together, to take them apart.

I stopped feeling afraid.

I stood in your office where the late–morning sun blazed, looking like it could incinerate every paper on your desk.

You turned to me as I pressed one finger on a thorny stitch through my clothes.

"Let's go for it," you said, already moving to grab the tools we needed. Obviously, you had considered the practicalities. I washed my hands. I waited, sitting in your office chair, big, black, able to tilt all the way back. Stripped down to panties, a bra—and ridiculously, my socks and boots—I sat rocking and swiveling, making eye contact as you took the stairs with your arms full of goodies.

I watched what you placed on a clean paper towel covering a rare clear spot on your desk. Rubbing alcohol, tissues, towels, Q–tips, a toe–nail clipper, tweezers, antibacterial cream, a small plastic spit pan, two kinds of scissors—one regular and one with an angle.

A tingle of fear shot through to my fingertips. You left to wash your hands and returned quickly.

"Who's cutting, you or me?"

"I want to give it a shot first," I said. "But you have to stay here and help."

"Oh, sure."

My butt slid forward to the edge of the chair. I assessed the degree of the stitch's curve against my body. I picked up the regular scissors, which you took from my hand to pour alcohol over them into the spit pan.

After you wiped and steadied them in my hand, I lowered the blade to the first stitch, not seeing how to cut without making a new incision. They shifted awkwardly in my hand. I put them down, sighing.

I realized that my line of vision kept catching a bulge of lace trim on my bra, so off it went, joining a pile of clothing on the floor.

I was holding my quad muscles so tightly that I had to stretch my legs, toes pointed.

"Okay," I said.

"Okay," you said.

I surveyed the makeshift instrument table.

"The toenail clipper might give you a good start. You can put the blunt edge right against your belly," you said.

"Good."

You poured alcohol over the clipper. I lined it up with the stitch, thought it looked fine, until I wondered aloud if I would catch the flesh of the incision beneath the clippers, the flesh closest to the pubic bone.

"Can you look?"

My voice sounded too chipper, someone else's voice.

"Well, you're adjusting a lot. I can't tell if it'll catch. Wait, lemme get a mirror."

I held my position like stone, the same pressure from my fingers on the clippers, its jaws suspended around the stitch, my backside at the heavily hemmed edge of your chair, knees bent akimbo. You bounded up the steps in seconds. You knelt between my knees, balancing the mirror on my pubic bone so that I could watch the other side of the clippers. You held it steady. I stopped shaking.

A clean, satisfying, metallic click.

You pulled the mirror away, cupped your hand beneath the clippers as I opened the jaws to drop the stitch.

"There it is," you said, delighted.

We peered at it, fascinated.

"Well, that's part of it—we have to pull this loop out all the way. That was just the knot on the outside," I said.

"Let's put alcohol and medicine on it before you pull it out."

"Good."

You dabbed with the alcohol, smeared the cream. I tensed with the cold of both. Nothing hurt. Alcohol went on the tweezers, which I lowered to the remains of the stitch.

"Want the mirror?" you said suddenly.

I jumped.

"No, I don't need it for this."

After the tweezers squeezed securely on the thread, I gave a little tug. I could feel it move in the skin.

"Hurt?"

"No, not really, but it feels strange."

"Should we leave it?"

"No, not this far along. We can't."

I pulled slowly, felt a faint tickle. I plunked the remainder of the white string on the paper towel, tweezers still in my fingers. We both stared at it. Then we looked in unison at my belly's two tiny holes where the stitch had been. Your smile, all teeth and gentleness.

"Well. That looks great."

"It does." I felt giddy.

"What about the other stitch?"

"I don't know why, but I don't feel like doing that one. Let's just leave it."

"Okay, another time. Enough surgery for today."

Days later, I told my dad what we did. Years later, I asked my dad what he thought about it.

"That was when I thought maybe you had gone goofy," he said.

"Really? I thought that was when I knew I could take on the world."

A letter to my ex about streams

Dear D.,

We considered route options after I spent another morning and evening white–knuckled on the steering wheel. The trip to and from the infusion suite lasted more than two hours from inevitable traffic embolisms all over the city. Even side roads swelled with clots of cars. We wondered if there were other travel routes. Maps did not encourage us. We had to make our way.

By the time I reached the suite, sometimes my veins had sabotaged the whole trip. No good veins, no blood work. Veins became both the road and the roadblock, more infuriating and essential than ratty city streets.

I dubbed you the designated hand–holder in my sickie kingdom while needles probed. I learned to squeeze tight. I did not breathe, did not make a sound until the feeling of threading beneath the skin stopped. Once I yelped when an IV broke through the vein, a high–pitched note like a clipped siren.

"Hush," you said under your breath.

I later learned what you told my parents: you thought I broke your hand during that visit.

You never made a sound.

$$\cdot\ \cdot\ \cdot\ \cdot\ \cdot\ \cdot$$

Blood work is work.

The nurses learn my quirks over the year, try to accommodate me. They knot the tourniquet over my pushed–up sleeve instead of directly on the skin. The nurse and I take turns poking at veins.

"There's a fatty. Go here," I say.

"I don't like the location," she says. "It will roll. What about this one?"

"That's so small. It's the smallest one. The needle will break through." Side streets were not available detours.

"Probably not. Bet I can hit it. I won't break through."

Her confidence wins me. I can't get medication I need without at least trying for blood, trying for veins. I grab your hand, my fingers through yours as I feel a butterfly needle threading through me. She wiggles the needle under the skin. I know the outcome.

"No good?"

"The vein is good. I hit it. I'm in. But there's no blood. You're so dehydrated."

I glance down.

"I can't take that movement under the skin with the needle. Pull out and stick again."

"If you say so."

I watch the silver pull out. Not a dot of blood followed.

"You're so dehydrated that you're not really bleeding."

"Let's try again. Maybe it was just that vein."

Maybe traffic will part like the Red Sea for me during rush hour on the drive home.

"Got any ideas?"

"Try any vein you want. I'm not helping this time."

Your fingers wriggle, readjust to grip again, already antic–
ipating the stick as much as I do. She's a good nurse with a
fairly painless entry. Once the needle moves back and forth
under the skin, I end it.

"No, that's just as bad, or else you would get some blood flow
by now."

"I'm sorry. I could get an oncology nurse to try it."

The needle pulls out, bloodless. Your hand releases with
perfect timing. If I hurt you, you never say. You eyes and
mouth stay as silent as your palms.

"No, it's not you because you actually hit the veins. If you
couldn't nail a vein, then I would try with another nurse. But
today seems to be me. I don't feel dehydrated, but maybe I'm
not paying attention."

I did not say, *my body and I take ongoing separate vacations
because this marriage isn't working out, but divorce is a cost I
can't take.*

I did not say, *I've taught myself how not to feel.*

I say, "I'll drink more next time. I can come back tomorrow."

On the drive home, traffic hemorrhages, clots, redirects its
pulsing, alternatively thins, thickens, rushes to wait. This is a
city where some drivers consider red lights optional. My grip
tightens, whitens to my fingertips.

At home, I pull two gauze pieces from non–bleeding non–
wounds. I'm tired at the end of the day, fried from fruitless
stress. My knuckles glare at me, a reddening lupus mess.

On one piece of paper, I want a map of feasible roads and feasible veins.

· · · · · ·

I wake early the next morning. I chug water and read until we're ready to leave. If we leave now, we beat morning rush hour. I bring a gallon of water with us in the car to sip.

Thirty minutes into the drive, my bladder screams. I try to keep a foot on the pedal as I involuntarily hunch. I pull off the main city artery to a fast food place.

"What are you doing?"

"Hopefully not wetting myself. Sit there."

I run with my thighs pressed together. My long winter coat covers my silly walk. When I pull on the door to no avail, a worker in uniform sees my distressed face.

"Nah! Not open! Early."

I grab the handle, yank compulsively. The door rattles. My bladder is decidedly unappreciative. I bring one leg up in a squeeze.

"Lady!" Both hands fly above the worker's head while his lips purse. The universal "what the fuck" sign. I've been served.

I run to the car with my gotta–pee run, realizing the drizzling rain is cold and a strong suggestion to my bladder. A block away, an abandoned building stands, once tall, majestic, busy and now a sturdy shell, useless.

"Where are we going? There's nothing here."

"There's privacy. I know what I'm doing."

"What are you doing?"

"I'm finding a way to go. This is not negotiable."

I drive into the forgotten lot of a forgotten building. Parked next to it, I can see the building's width is enormous. I feel reassured.

I reach for the tissue box on the back seat, grab a wad. I sit in the driver's seat unbuttoning my shirt, unzipping my jeans.

The scenario clicks for you suddenly.

"No. You're not."

"Got other options to go?"

A groan.

"Just sit here and don't come out. I mean it. I've done this before under other emergency conditions."

I am not dehydrated.

"I've got a way."

I am practical and ridiculous.

I shut the door, stalk toward the rear tire closest to the building. Under my coat, I ease my jeans and granny panties to my knees as I lower into a wide–legged squat. I try to disperse my weight evenly across the soles of both feet. My nose hovers two inches from the treads. I pull my coat around to create my own stall while I finger the treads, carefully examining a tire problem that does not exist.

I am very much not dehydrated.

This better be the goriest blood test ever.

I consciously relax, grip the tire with both hands, hear the first splats of a stream against decrepit concrete. I've chosen an exceptionally good spot: urine floods toward the uneven opening of a pothole, pools there. Bereft motor oil makes broken, shifting rainbows as urine steams its way through them.

I use the tissues, contribute to the litter, and feel gratitude in my body.

My hand uses the tire for support as I heave out of an extended squat while my other hand simultaneously yanks my jeans and underwear upward. Forgotten in this maneuver is the length of the coat, which dips solidly into pee, rain water, the last emissions of cars long gone.

I don't think. On reflex, I stand at an awkward angle to keep the coat's edge away while pushing my hands into the pockets to check for my belongings. I retrieve gloves. In a record quick shrug, my coat lands on the now–filled pothole. I dart to the car.

"Forgot something?" You already giggling.

"Nope. I feel so much better."

"For real, where's your coat?"

"Abandoned."

A huge smirk. "Whhhhhhhyyyyyy?"

"Don't irritate the driver. Look at this traffic."

"Yeah. Well. Someone couldn't make the whole trip before rush hour busted out. Wow, you must be cold."

"No. I'm too warmed by my victory. I didn't wet myself. Score."

Laughter. "My, my, how the mighty have fallen."

Silence, obscenities at traffic, pee jokes occupy the long tedium in the car.

· · · · · ·

At the infusion suite, I feel confident.

Jennifer Clare Burke

"I heard about yesterday," the nurse says. She does not feel confident. It's her first time sticking me.

"How do you feel today? Hydrated?"

"Yes, really hydrated," I say as you laugh loudly, which begets a puzzled smile from the nurse.

"Okay, let me get the stuff and a tech, just in case."

She returns with supplies, a towel, a tech. The tourniquet pops veins I didn't know I had.

"That's a parking lot!" exclaims the tech, looking at the patchwork of veins. You laugh loudly again as you take my hand. "The nurse has lots of places to go. You have a lot of good ones," the tech goes on. I'm surprised when I look at my arm.

"Just to be sure," the nurse says, "I'm going to put your arm on this towel so you stay anchored." Her hands contour a hot towel as a base under my elbow and arm.

"I'm usually pretty still," I insist. Her glance at your hand gripping mine indicates disbelief.

"Okay then. Let's get started."

Cold wetness, brisk rubbing, the sharp stink of alcohol.

The sight of swollen veins—many of them—makes me queasy. I twist, turn full face to you, watching your eyes watching my arm. My hand grabs hard at yours with the sting of a needle. Not a second later, disgust, shock, color your face as I feel strange warm wetness emerge over the length of my forearm.

"Ooopsie, we made a mess! Wasn't expecting that."

An arc of blood has literally shot out of my arm with enough force to coat my arm to my wrist, dribbling to the floor and my jeans.

"Sorry about your clothes. That should come out if you dab as soon as we finish here. You've got a real live one here."

As she draws another tube of blood, her other hand takes the edge of the towel to dab my arm. I intentionally do not look until she has assured me that everything is clean of blood, the wet towel balled under her arm.

"You know, I'm just going to throw this out."

She deposits the bloody towel into the biohazard trash. Your hand releases my hand.

"It's like your blood couldn't wait to jump out of your body and go some place else," you say.

"I don't blame my blood. I'll have to throw out my jeans. She made light of it, but that's a big stain. And how can I treat it now while I drive home?"

Laughter again. "Why should that stop you?"

A letter to my ex about craving

Dear D.,

Only you can find truths in carbohydrates.

"Are you kissing me this much because I just ate garlic bread that you're not allowed to eat?"

"Yes."

A letter to my ex about belly noises

Dear D.,

Years ago, we didn't know that my stomach was on its last legs. It was obvious, but we hoped for the best.

My stomach was a wayward pet needing to be cajoled into good behavior. Perhaps it could be housebroken, taught better habits. We tried.

You stocked the freezer with tortellini and chicken, put cans of tuna in the cabinets, horded soda for me. We hoped some more.

We both knew that I didn't want the trouble of eating unless I absolutely had to endure it. My weight became a problem as my bones achieved greater definition. Digestion was the enemy, bringing more problems than starving.

I decided to be willfully obtuse about the realities of some bodily failings. You never judged me on those failings from the start, but you wouldn't let me cheat reality either.

I skipped meals when nausea troubled me too badly. Flesh melted.

You started sneaking food into bed, eating next to me, hoping I would steal bits from your plate.

"Mmmmmm. Cheese and turkey all rolled up."

I put my head under the pillow.

"Bleck."

"I know you're really hungry."

"I know I'll really puke it."

At night and at dawn, my stomach screeched and gurgled like a dying dog choking on its blood. This description is not so far from the truth of what happened later in the emergency room, after I left you. That was the night of a troublesome esophageal tear from puking so much, and fear, fear, fear when nurses wouldn't allow sips of water. It was the night of sitting upright in the gurney, shaking wrists on side railings; of more pukes into a plastic, mustard yellow bin; of seeing elongated bubbles of ripe, fatty blood floating on bile.

· · · · · ·

There were always three of us in bed: you, me, and the raging beastie of my belly, punctuating its hostile bellows with curly, beseeching moans.

"Jesus," you said, the second voice in the dark.

"Ummrrhh," I said, trying to sleep through it.

Under the covers, giggles and commentary came with each noise.

"Ooooo, just like a floorboard."

"Beg pardon? Did you say something over there?"

"That was like nails on a chalkboard."

"Can't some exotic species of bird make that sound, too?"

"It's so very impressive, isn't it?"

Sometimes you put your head on my stomach to listen.

"Whoooaa," you said.

"I know," I said.

A letter to my ex about fallout

Dear D.,

Sometimes we don't know what was in the air filling our lungs. We don't know what really touched us, what stayed behind to change us forever.

In the morning, we decided to ditch work for a half–day of people–watching at the fountain, the biggest one in the park that had become our favorite. We walked through the dense neighborhoods from your apartment to the center of town where the art museums, restaurants and the park converged.

The hiss of a bus door closing caught my ear. I turned in time to see it push laboriously past me. Bus exhaust clung to my clothes, I was sure, even though I couldn't see smudges. I swore I could lick the fabric of my shirt to taste it—if I tried, which I never did. You would have been horrified at such an act in public, despite my justifiable curiosity.

I stifled that urge. I tried to stifle another one around you on these walks: I felt the need to pee once the sound of the fountain became distinguishable above the white–noise rumbles of traffic and people.

"Then stop having coffee before we leave for a walk!" you said.

Your ears weren't connected to your bladder. You didn't understand this problem. I experienced an immediate connection between sound waves and the body.

Once we reached the fountain, we found a spot on the ledge to settle next to each other, not touching but close. Kids shrieked, seemingly chaotically, until we sat for a while. Then we caught the rhythm: churning water, shooting sprays in half–assed choreography, with the cadence of name–calling and hoots as people—and the occasional dog—jumped in the water, whooping with every wide–legged step.

Water sloshed on our thighs as fountain crashers propelled waves. Hypnotic percussion: a yelp, a splash, a sound of water hitting skin and pavement. Out of chaos, order. Rhythm, rhythm everywhere.

"I feel better," you said.

"Didja feel bad earlier? I never knew. I didn't hear you say anything."

"I wasn't feeling bad earlier. I'm just better *now*. All those ions hitting me—that's why."

Your face turned up, focused on the arc shooting across the circumference of the fountain.

"Ions?"

"Fountains release ions. You absorb them from the falling water. They affect you. They're these little bits of electricity roaming in the air, bouncing off you, changing your electrical field. Your mood changes."

I said nothing. Water droplets bounced from our knees to the ground. Another dog jumped in the water, biting the shooting jets. Call–and–response rhythm with each nip.

"It's all scientific," you said to the silence.

"Which means it's true."

"Yes. Don't you feel better? Don't you think it has to be true?"

I could smell exhaust from traffic not so far away swirling with freshness from the spraying water. I could smell the sunscreen worn by the woman on my other side each time she moved.

"I think fountains cause release, yes. I need a bathroom. I always have to pee near fountains. You know that."

"How much coffee did you have?"

"We do not blame coffee for anything. Coffee is always good. It's the ions doing this to me. They affect people, you said."

I eased off the fountain's ledge to make my usual path to the makeshift row of portable potties while you sat, sucking on ions.

I prepared myself with wads of tissue stuffed in my purse. I wouldn't have to touch a single questionable potty surface. There would always be some atoms between the potty's ominous surfaces and my vulnerable surfaces.

With a tissue acting as a chainmail glove, I pulled the potty door open, stepping only on my toes after checking for puddles. I pulled the door shut with the same tissued hand. The light inside the putrid box wasn't working. It should have lit as soon as the door latched. Ugh. I made a quilt of wadded tissues and hovered near the rim.

Then relief. Finally relief. With only a paper cut of daylight through the ceiling's joints, everything in the potty was blurry, contours shifting between shadow and substance. I let my eyes go out of focus while I listened to my private fountain. I wondered if ions were crawling through the air. Pee was falling water, after all.

When I stepped out, sunlight blinded me. The fountain's multiple percussion sections took center stage in my ears. I sat next to you again, neither of us looking at each other nor speaking.

A child jumped in, fell forward, the sound of shallow water flatly breaking against his chest. One enormous jet shot its way across the top of the fountain, one end to the other, churning the water underneath to whiteness. I thought of ejaculate, life.

Another stream shot from the center to the ledge, cresting, losing force, dribbling back into pooling bubbles beneath it. Another dog took turns biting undulating jets. Two more kids splashed each other.

Water droplets collected on our bare thighs. The rotation of these events changed, yet we could predict which rhythm would happen next.

"Feel better now?" you asked.

"Yes. My bladder is environmentally suggestible. I do what I gotta do."

I let my fingers skim the water's surface.

"Environmentally suggestible?"

You sneering but nice.

"It's very scientific."

Me sneering but not nice.

"Do you know what an ion is?"

"I'm sure I did in high school. I never knew that they liked to congregate around fountains—kind of like a singles bar?"

"Ions are about attraction, yes. And they're a mix of positive and negative."

The sun and heat peaked; we knew my outdoor time was up. Immunosuppressives did not mingle well with sunlight and warm temperatures. You had work waiting for you. I had treatment.

· · · · · ·

Jennifer Clare Burke

When the automatic doors of the hospital's main entrance sighed open, the smell hit: shampooed carpets, disinfected floors, old plastic chairs, generic detergent, something synthetic but unascertainable, something stale and too human. The lobby presented a moving, rhythmic obstacle course of people in scrubs, nurses in pastels, patients in wheelchairs.

In the infusion center's waiting room, a woman took a chair next to mine.

"You're very young," she said.

I smiled, closed lips.

"There's gonna be a wait today. I can see that," she said.

I nodded, silent.

"What cancer are you here for?"

"No cancer. Lupus. Regular maintenance stuff. It's a much lower dose of medication."

My diagnosis leaped through the air, shooting in an arc, bouncing off her face.

"I had ovarian cancer, or still do, I dunno. But my doctor says he caught it in time. I should be okay."

I looked closely: her eyelashes and eyebrows were evaporated. She wore a wig, hyper–pink lipstick, a loose dress. As I inclined slightly toward her, she said something about next week's treatment schedule and her son–in–law.

I heard none of it.

I had leaned close enough to inhale her breath, to taste it. There it was, the stench I recognized: disease, treatment, speckling her mouth with molecules of the battlefield that was her body.

She spoke more, air leaving her lips. I feared taking in molecules of scorched earth from the intensity of her chemotherapy and radiation.

"…it's supposed to be some kind of pulse therapy, so I'm not sure exactly which days I come in," she said, grateful to be talking.

A pinpoint of her spittle landed on my jaw. I felt it.

Immediately I pushed the air out of my mouth forcefully. It sounded like a sigh but felt like dodging death. I pictured mushroom clouds floating above each of her white cells, poison radiating from each like sound waves. I grabbed a tissue from my purse, swiped it across my jaw.

"Oh, I think my name was called," I lied, balled the tissue in my hand. I made my way to a different part of the waiting room near the sign–in counter.

I spent the remainder of my visit swishing Coke, water and my saliva around my mouth, exhaling deeply.

I could hear your voice in my head, penetrating my mood: "You absorb them. They affect you. It's scientific."

I drove home with all four windows open in the car, your words in my pores. I could replay your voice. I could even hear the whooshing of the fountain in the background, a perfectly recorded sound bite.

Immediately I had to pee.

Great. I did it to myself.

When I pulled into your driveway, you were home from work. I hadn't realized how long the day had been in treatment. I bolted from the car, up the stairs, straight through the doorway where you stood waiting.

"Hey," you started, hands extended to me.

Jennifer Clare Burke

"Nope, nope, gotta pee!"

I left the bathroom door slightly ajar while commencing business quickly.

"Yeah," you said, shuffling outside the bathroom door.

I could hear your socks brushing against the carpet as I finished and tore my clothes off while seated. I rushed to the shower, turning the knobs full force. The knobs were inches from the door—you heard me.

"Right now?" you said, gently pushing the door open with only your fingertips, as if fingertips caused less intrusion, less insistence.

"I thought we would hang out for a bit, maybe have dinner now, then watch tv."

"We can, but I need ions first. It won't take long."

From where I stood, you slid through the door to stand close to me. I could reach both you and the faucets. I put my right arm under the water to check the temperature. I wrapped my left arm around your waist, pulled you to my face. I sniffed your shirt collar, sweater, hair. I didn't wait for your reaction as I felt the temperature adjust on my right hand.

I stepped into the shower and kept breathing deeply.

A letter to my ex about meat packing

Dear D.,

We had already performed surgery together.

We pulled a stitch from my belly after the incision healed. Another stitch remained.

I would have saved the stitch for the appointment with the surgeon, but it itched horribly. Larger than the removed stitch, it hung lower, catching on my jeans and making me gasp.

You flopped on the bed, flipping channels while I showered. When I walked into the bedroom, I dripped still–warm water under my robe.

"This last one has to go," I said. "Let's take it out."

You knew already what I was talking about.

"Not when you're wet. It'll be easier once it's totally dry."

"Good."

I walked to the kitchen to make lasagna for us, as promised. I grabbed my pan, spatula, ladle, wondering which tools to use on my remaining stitch. Last time, you set the instrument table. Now it was my turn. What to use, what to use.

I cut pasta to fit the pan. I chopped vegetables, peeled skins. I sliced meat. I thought the layers of slash–red tomato and soft pasta resembled the meat inside my belly.

I thought more about my incision, the stuff underneath. When I woke from the operation, the surgeon's white coat merged with the brightness of many overhead fluorescent lights until my eyes adjusted. She explained that my organs rested so out of place that she repacked my abdomen, much like organizing a haphazard suitcase.

The second the anesthesia abated, I knew I was ordered again. The surgeon was right. My entire trunk felt different, less stressed, now harmonic. I twisted in the gurney in the recovery room toward her when she spoke. For the first time in years, there was no pain, no sense of being pulled apart from the inside. I pressed the edges of the pasta to make the filling even and slipped the pan in the oven.

"Ready now?" you called.

I went to the bathroom, pawing through the cabinet for tools. I found very small scissors with tiny, sharp tips that I used to shape my eyebrows. They would do. I took antibiotic cream, rubbing alcohol, gauze pads.

"Oh, we don't have your nifty office chair." I stopped.

I hadn't considered the location for our next surgery. I placed my tools on the edge of the sink next to the toilet.

"Do you want to use the mirror like last time?"

"Yes. We might as well just do it in here. I want to sit again, with you on your knees to help me."

"Yeah, you would want that."

You left to snatch a hand mirror from the bedroom, still snorting. Me so toppy.

I sat on the toilet, my robe half on. I leaned back until my shoulder blades touched the tank, extended my legs, feet

Jennifer Clare Burke

resting on the ledge of the tub. I rocked around a bit to see my abdomen from different angles.

"I know what I want to do here," I said, taking the mirror from your hands as you settled on the floor between my legs. "If you sit on the floor instead of kneeling, I can rest my feet on your shoulders while you hold the mirror. I think the angle will be perfect."

"This is easier on my knees," you said.

"Good."

"Good."

You swabbed the entire incision and the scissors with alcohol. Like last time, you put medicine on the stitch. Then you balanced the mirror again on my pubic bone as my feet pressed into the outermost edges of your collarbones.

"Your feet are so cold."

The tip of the scissors slid under the knot with little guidance. I checked the mirror's reflection to see if I would snip the elevated flesh of the incision. Everything looked clear.

I heard the crunchy slice of the stitch. Not like last time with one clear, decisive snip. I realized I hadn't cut through all the way. The stitch remained intact by a filament.

I shifted my feet on your shoulders. You said nothing. The scissors weren't as sharp as I thought.

I lined up the tip with the suture, checked the mirror, pressed. One end of the stitch immediately fell into my belly, underneath my flesh. I didn't feel a tickle. You grabbed the other side with your fingers to pull it.

My first sensation: air hitting the minuscule holes that remained. Then I saw the brownish red smudge on the stitch between your fingers.

"Guess I'll cancel the appointment with the surgeon."

I put my feet on the floor, sat up.

"Is the lasagna ready?"

I looked at the blood on the stitch in your hand before you tossed it in the garbage.

A letter to my ex about possession

Dear D.,

The body didn't intimidate or shame you—not mine, anyhow.

You were matter–of–fact, careful about everything with
the body: bad morning breath, grit beneath your nails from
playing with engines, my sweaty hair, rancid laundry.

You never laughed at the ridiculous imprint my pantyhose
seam made across my belly after I peeled them off in a
laughable series of contortions so my nails wouldn't pull a
run.

· · · · · ·

It was your idea. You were ready.

You would make dinner, getting everything for this night,
which was all about your efforts, about me being in your home
for the first time. Mostly this night was about pleasing me,
which embarrassed but delighted me: it mattered to you how I
thought of you, if I thought you could make me happy or care
about nitpicky things that made me relaxed for no reason. I
know that you did. I knew then, too. I don't know if I showed
it.

I had never stayed overnight at your home before; in fact,
I had never been to your home at all. In preparation, you
moved furniture around in your living room so that you
could throw a mattress on the floor with pillows before the

television. Why? Because I said my most comfortable spot was always on a mat or a mattress on the floor, no matter where I lived or stayed; that was where I ate, did work, napped. You hauled the mattress from your bedroom onto the floor downstairs to make me comfortable.

When I arrived, my hair dripped a darkened spot on my shirt because I didn't own a hair dryer. You sat in knots. I wore my hair loose, wet whips swaying below my hips, sticking to things, including you, like exploring tentacles. You had never felt that before.

I could see it in your face, in the starch in your pants' creases: they were as stiff as your shoulders. The butterflies had not changed from the teen years.

You had two sets of bouquets for me, two different types of flowers you thought I would like. One was roses; another was tulips. You had two movies ready for that night. One movie I don't remember. I sat through it, thinking mostly about whether I was nervous or not, what you expected of me.

The other was *The Exorcist*, digitally re–mastered, my favorite. I was thrilled you were willing to sit through a Catholic horror movie, one you found incredibly stupid. Perhaps the power of Christ compelled you, perhaps you loved me even then. I didn't think there was such a thing as a bad possession movie that involved the throwing of holy water. You were willing to tolerate my taste in corny brands of evil.

Little did we know what foreshadowing Linda Blair's pea–soup spew would hold for that evening.

You bought shrimp for that night, some special kind. I can't remember what kind of preparation the store did, what you did. You were proud because procuring them took some wrangling over the Labor Day weekend that had temperature lows around ninety–eight degrees.

The heat had set records for the entire month and a half. We were already acquainted with the smell of each other's sweat by the time we finished introducing ourselves in a gym; that was when we said hello for the third time, actually stopping to talk because I had caught you staring at my ass. It was obvious enough that you were trying not to be a pig, but you failed. We both laughed.

You told me about driving over an hour in one direction to the fish place, one you didn't know well, had never used before. Everything else was closed over the holiday weekend. For over an hour as you came home, the seafood sat in your truck without ice, without any protection from record heat, save for your air conditioner.

A more sturdy soul with a less moody belly could have stomached this concoction, but I wasn't that person. I didn't mention this fact. I did my best to ignore it. You had just sat through an excellent day for an exorcism without snorting or groaning, even during the x–ray scenes.

I waited on the mattress while you went to the kitchen. You returned with one large plate. Something looked too raw about the shrimp. I didn't know what, didn't ask questions. Your face was painfully pleased. I didn't want to say no.

I said, "You first."

"You don't want any?" Eyes wide, eyebrows raised. Genuine alarm.

I wanted to start laughing. I didn't. I tap danced.

"Oh, yes, yes, I will. I just never had them . . . prepared this way." This was English for "I–am–so–fucking–horrified–right–now–but–let's–not–be–ugly–everything–will–be–fine."

You took a huge bite, seemed okay, but you were big, ridiculously strong, one of the Not–Sick People. At first, I thought you would never understand my life, my body, for this very reason. You kept staying, waiting, hearing me, so I was sitting on your mattress.

"They're great."

You pushed the plate toward me. I picked one, didn't look at it, and bit a little. Seemed okay. Had another. Maybe everything would be fine. We finished off the plate.

"You liked them?"

"Oh yes. Thanks."

You put the plate on the table on your side of the mattress. I leaned back on the pillows with you. My hair, now dry, hung loose.

"Wanna stay to watch the news?" Your hand was on the remote.

"Okay."

I leaned over to bite your shoulder, to mess your perfect hair. You didn't jump. I felt your chest move very slowly, as if you fought to make air stay in your lungs. You didn't fight me, so I rolled on top of you, resting my forehead against your neck. I felt a little worn out but not bad.

Your hands touched everywhere over my clothes. The news droned on. There was stillness and possibility between us, full of newness, restraint.

I froze. I felt it. The first pang, unmistakable, squeezing on the left side of my belly. My vision swirled, my lids heavy, my body so slow. I knew you noticed right away, too. I rolled off you quickly, half lying, half sitting on my side of the mattress. The weather forecaster monotoned new records full of heat, a warning for heavy thunderstorms full of noise. I was bracing.

You knew I had lupus. You knew I had no remissions and some funky drugs. You didn't know entirely what that all meant, including the secondary problems now established as part of my life, like my belly's inability to contain itself.

I stayed in silence wondering if the pains, the spinning would stop. I didn't know what to say.

Jennifer Clare Burke

You stayed quiet for a bit, thankfully unmoving. Only your eyes followed me steadily as I moved off you to my space on the mattress. You blinked. Something already apologetic in your eyes. You weren't embarrassed. For that, I was relieved.

"Somethin's burnin'," you said.

Now I had to say something. "I don't think I'm okay."

"Are you upset? Did I do something wrong back there?"

"No, sick." I grabbed my belly.

"Oh no."

"Yeah."

I was already standing up but bent over.

"I could take care of you here if you're not okay."

You weren't just being polite.

"You've done enough for me tonight. I think I should go."

I bolted toward the table to grab my flowers, flew toward the door, pecking you on the cheek, not worrying if that was insulting. My stomach did not take kindly to the shrimp. I had taken all my meds. I wasn't in much pain at all anywhere in my body. It had to be dinner.

That was another of many signs that my food intake would change thanks to a nasty hospitalization with time spent on the "hostage chic" diet, complete with plain rice, water, boiled meat, wide absences. I didn't know that then, didn't realize it was serious, something developing to alter my life even more.

You weren't fazed.

"Call me as soon as you get in."

You were standing in the doorway watching me dodge to my car, parked in the street. My stomach flip–flopped in between cramping. I gagged, swallowed before my key unlocked the door. I drove home in the far right lane in case I had to pull over. Thankfully the drive was short.

Once I made it to the safety of my driveway, I leaned out of the car, felt the inevitable begin.

Yet another barf into my neighbor's begonias. I bet they wondered how that flowerbed died.

So much for seafood.

My legs were gelatin before I reached my door. I hung over the bathroom sink, breathed for a while as I rinsed my mouth. I thought the nausea was lifting. I simply wasn't eating certain foods anymore. That much was obvious. At least I didn't need the emergency room for that night.

The phone rang.

"Are you okay?"

"Well, I just lost dinner, but I feel okay now."

"As long as you feel better. Was it the shrimp, you think?"

"Eh. Maybe. Food and I don't always get along, you know. I think that's just part of my deal at this point."

"Oh."

"I don't think you poisoned me, if that's what you're asking."

You laughing, again. "Now that you feel okay, you wanna come back?"

"Are you serious? Tonight?"

"Yes! I won't make you eat food, I promise."

Jennifer Clare Burke

There was the promise you would break, time and time again, as I grew more ill, as I tied my hair back more often, as you stopped eating, too.

A letter to my ex about road rage

Dear D.,

A psychologist once explained to me that after loss, we
continue looking for the lost love object. I never looked for
you, but I did see you on some days more than others. I was
hunting for lost shadows in an empty room: I only saw myself.

My friend, W., planned her major surgery. She asked me to
babysit her afterward for a four–hour shift on each of four
days. I knew sickie stuff well. By that point, I had been
diagnosed and treated for over a year. She felt safe because
she knew that while healing, she could do nothing to scare or
to disgust me.

Before her surgery, I arrived at her home to learn the security
codes, to practice opening tricky locks with recently copied,
rough–edged keys. I scrawled code numbers in my notepad,
practiced punching each one until a white light glowed with
a beep. I knew every code, every lock in the house. I could
get in anywhere with no problem. W. and I were satisfied. I
buttoned my coat and started my car.

Her suburban development held itself together with twisting,
misleading streets, everywhere a cul–de–sac. Every path
seemed to promise a way to the main road, but I was thrown
back into the maze repeatedly, lost again.

I kept driving, trying to find a way out. My internal compass
spun to reorient as each new angle made the roads look

different. Trying to get out brought confusion, false starts. After I threw the car into reverse, I made yet another three-point turn in a dead end. I headed in a new direction that seemed to be the right path. I thought it would lead to the main road ahead.

I had to go home.

Before I reached the main road, a car cut in front of me from one of the side streets. The car proceeded until it stopped suddenly dead, inches from my front bumper. I slammed on my brakes as hard as I could, felt the force radiate from ankle to knee. All my papers and books on the seats thudded to the floor. The car ahead stayed still. No blinker lights, no turn signal, no signs. The road was too narrow for me to pull around.

I waited.

The driver's door opened. I primed myself to lean out the window and yell. I saw the person more clearly.

I thought it was you.

The cussing jammed in my throat. As the driver walked around the front of the car, I took in the profile. Not you.

The driver stepped onto the sidewalk, placing a handful of letters into a mailbox I never noticed. I might as well have been broad-sided. Full impact. I never saw you coming.

I had left you. That was it. Then there was an errant car, a driver mailing letters, and there you were, resurrected, Lazarus standing in newly constructed suburbs in late February.

My hands hurt from choking the wheel. My neck started to spasm from how hard I locked my jaws together to keep from repeating your name to the driver. I needed to go home. My car was not invisible. Clearly I wanted to move on the road. The driver settled into the car slowly, starting it,

Jennifer Clare Burke

shifting clothing, adjusting the seat belt, rustling through something on the passenger side, generally being a self–centered ass.

Despite irritation, I was thrilled: the stranger gave me more time to stare. My body held the feeling that comes with the highest point of the roller coaster: the biggest drop about to happen, that nanosecond of an eyeful of the way down, the point before screaming registers.

I waited for the stranger to drive. I followed.

I watched the driver's rear–view mirror to see if I recognized your eyes, if maybe it really was you. I followed farther away from W.'s cushy suburbs where the complicated, perfect homes resembled gingerbread houses, a neighborhood of simulacra.

There are the things I never said since we started talking again, D. This is one of them.

For a while after The Big Split, we spoke a bit, until we decided to exist in silence, apart. During the talking period, you confessed to me the time you saw me driving on Route 76 while you drove in the opposite direction. You nearly crashed, trying to watch my car in your mirrors. You said you were ruined for the day, useless.

I pretended I had no idea what you meant. I didn't want to know the effects of loss. I stayed silent, not to be cruel, but to make things fade like taillights on the highway.

I drove, following the stranger. I wasn't near the suburbs anymore. I followed until I saw long stretches of untended fields, unpainted old houses, increasingly small strip malls of cheap stores, and occasional churches—I saw "SALVATION" painted grossly on more than one church's sign. These bits of civilization grew father apart.

I was following a stranger who mailed letters in a posh development, who drove for miles into the periphery where wilderness ruled. Miles out, I knew you weren't there. If I followed any longer, I wouldn't find my way back. I made a left turn, pulled into the parking lot of a store that closed early because it was Sunday.

In the lot, I thought about W.'s belly being cut open, all the ways she found to keep people out of her home, her life, all those codes and keys. I thought of the not–you stranger who hogged the road without looking at me. I cried hard enough in the car that my sides hurt. I briefly considered if I would be able to shift gears to drive home.

I smeared snot all over the steering wheel, wiped it with my sleeves, feeling disgusted, satisfied.

I opened the windows. All the air in the car was missing, my lungs a black hole in my body, chasing after everything, sucking down anything, even a fake version of you.

My shoulders ached. I wondered about my medication schedule. I still had time before my next dose, so I sat longer, watching the sky change to dark red, violet. Nothing moved in the parking lot, except late day shifted to night. March was coming. I could already smell changes in the air telling me the earth was ready. I glanced to the edge of the parking lot where the apparently dead trees leaned against each other. Spring would change everything.

I realized, sitting there, two things. One, that this spring would see you gone; it felt like a limb had been ripped away in an ugly accident. Two, that I was late for dinner when I had promised to be there on time.

I turned the key in the ignition, knowing it was time to go home again, time to let changes happen. I left the windows open. My eyes looked like two bloated cherry tomatoes. My nose wasn't much better.

My seatbelt bit into my ribs. Pink, then darkening blue, streaked the sky. I randomly entertained images in my head of bruises, of flesh inside your lower lip, of all the compromises I didn't make, not because I was proud, but because I believed freedom was more fragile than cracked eggshells.

The wind blew strongly into the car, drying my face until I came home. My lips cracked, leaving feathery veins of blood across my teeth.

A letter to my ex about zombies

Dear D.,

Some things just don't die. They keep visiting in different forms over and over. Their vitality might not be there, but the familiarity is. You exist in ink now. I play with memories and possibility on page after page. I make paper dolls of us, cutting our shapes, telling stories over and over.

You and I used to talk about my dreams. You could never remember what you dreamed. I never saw any evidence that you dreamed at all when I watched your body, leaden with sleep, unmoving. When I woke up, I yapped right away, still half asleep, slurring, trying to catch the narrative from my dream as it evaporated from my lids.

I don't remember the last dream I had with you lying next to me. I don't remember the last one I described to you as I woke.

But I do remember the dream after you left.

I'm in a small town, a place peopled with many neighbors whom I know well, a place with a long history of traditions. People prepare for Daemon Day, a big holiday. Daemon Day is yet another holiday where I am forced to socialize with a bunch of people for no justifiable reason. It grows tedious. I prefer to socialize where and when I want, when I'm ready.

I know everything about Daemon Day as well as I know the pattern of veins looping over the backs of your hands and the tops of your feet. "Daemon" also means "demon," which has come to refer to an evil spirit.

Daemon Day does not take its cue from that meaning, not in this town. *Daemon* is the genius we find in ourselves, usually whatever we fight hardest against, try to destroy, but eventually integrate as part of the self. Maybe this happens in every relationship where love comes...and goes.

Here, people keep rituals around Daemon Day and Daemon Day Eve. On the Eve, schools let out early. People make plans for the next twenty–four hours. One event is a huge picnic and a gathering around a pool.

I attend for a while, swim laps, eat, talk. I remain halfhearted, wanting to go home to be with my thoughts. People encourage, almost insist, that I stay. This is where the truth starts to reveal itself in other people's wisdom and fears.

I stand on the edge of the pool, watching the late afternoon disappear, speaking to a circle of people in the water.

"I'm ready to go. This is making me tired. I'm ready to go it alone this year."

"But you can't leave. Everyone will be okay if we stay together. Tomorrow only really becomes a Daemon Day if you're alone tonight. That's when it happens. Anyhow, there's the all–nighter party after the barbecue for dinner. No one should be alone."

"Do you really believe this?"

"Do you really not believe it? We have the holiday for a reason."

"I don't think anyone gets saved in the end," I say, believing myself.

With that, I turn and leave, walking home, resolving that my fate is my own, that I can't—shouldn't—use other people as a buffer. If something is after me, I can only run so far. It will find me. It will keep coming back.

Daemon Day Eve, my ass. At home, I cook dinner and watch tv as late–night talk shows air.

I hear a pedestrian, almost friendly knock on the door. A shot goes from my chest to my feet. A snarling zombie, ready to hack incisors into my neck.

So be it.

I pull the unlocked door open. There you are, relaxed.

"Hey," you smile.

Nothing bad happens. You peer over my shoulder. You don't have fangs or an exposed skull.

"Is someone here?" you ask.

No flesh–eating monsters. You're laughing already.

"You're gonna let me in, right?"

Your head bobs "yes" as you ask. It's you, goofy, familiar. Am I supposed to be afraid? You're all charm and normalcy, like you always arrive at two a.m. when I thought you were lost to me in this life.

You're here. What's so bad about Daemon Day? This is heaven. You're back. There's no work to redeem myself, to return to a place where we once were. I'm a believer. This is my moment of changing from Saul to Paul not in the light but in the 2 a.m. darkness. This is Daemon Day. You even smell like you.

You slide past me in the doorway, hands still in your jacket pockets. You make your way to my bed. You're still smiling as you sit down on it.

"Oh, come on," you say.

That's all it takes.

I'm yours because you're here. That's how I have my night with you. Or something that seemed like you, or something I thought was you.

That night, my body automatically molds to the shape of you, the space you need to sleep, the way you like the quilt arranged. I can feel your hair tickle my neck. You forget to remove your watch as you usually do before bed; the cold metal occasionally bites into my flesh.

The first thing I hear in the morning is a bird chirping, so loudly and clearly that I'm concerned. I open my eyes to see it resting on the curtain rod. I feel cold air on my arms. A strong breeze comes through the open front door.

Didn't we close it last night?

You're gone.

There's no smell of you, no imprint of your head on the pillow, not a hair left behind, not a footprint, a thread. I don't have to wonder if you are at the table, in the kitchen or shower. I know with the force of a head–on collision that you are gone.

I'm crazy, maybe possessed, after all. I'm alone with a bird. With the realization, I feel the complete absence of pain anywhere. Then it hits, coring pain. The bird sings, its head moving at different angles to watch me. You came back; maybe you were never here. I don't know, don't need to know when this pain is the bottom line from a zombie attack.

Time slows, becomes tangible, woolly, as I move through it, trying to explain in my head what happened. The people at the party were not afraid of night, of Daemon Day Eve, of monsters, of death. They were not afraid of meeting their daemons and inviting them inside.

They were afraid of their daemons leaving the next morning when they would be left only with themselves. They were not afraid of being torn to pieces by the returning undead, but by being hollowed out by loss anew.

You're gone. It is this moment, in the morning sunshine of Daemon Day, not last night's seduction at the door, that is my true conversion.

• • • • • •

I wake, trying to ward off zombies.

Afterward

I'm the one who became a dancing ball of light, and D. is someone else

Who is D.?

D. isn't here.

That's the important thing to know because it's the reason these letters exist. There is no annotated version of how love and the diseased body take the flight of Icarus together.

D. is not one person, but multiple ex–partners who had an almost Gestalt impact on how I saw myself and the world. They reminded me then and now of gentleness in other people and the power to experience the world through touching skin. I took pieces of different individuals' personalities and slivers of different experiences with each.

I could have chosen any alphabet letter for the initial in each salutation. "D." doesn't stand for anything in particular, though now I could say that it stands for "Dear Destroyer," as each person ruined my preconceptions and gave me a different sense of self. I don't consider the moniker "Destroyer" to be anything close to an insult.

It makes perfect sense to me that I keep writing to an apparently unchanging D. because, in essence, each time I find the same person, make the same mistakes and try to master the same traumas. I'm not sure if that period of development is over in my life or if awareness vanquishes demons. I suspect that relationship demons constitute another type of chronic illness that is managed day to day with varying levels of commitment and different definitions of "problem," "success" and "cure."

A Life Less Convenient is fiction because in the writing, I intended to tell dishonest narratives to reach my truths. I changed facts, including location, the timing of events and other elements of the stories. These changes enable the narrative to flow and also to keep identities anonymous. Why? Mostly to protect us from ourselves, because no one in this book is innocent or guilty.

I could have spelled out names, given more specific time sequences or created fully representational pictures. I could have written this story completely differently, and someday I might do that. For now, I am the subjectivity, present with my flawed sense of perspective and my inability to see from D.'s point of view.

D. is not the writer here. I am.

When I was a child, someone asked me what I wanted to be when I grew up. I told the truth that D. intuitively understood: I wanted to be a dense ball of spinning, bright light that never sat still, hot enough to be white, a fire that kept burning with no fuel and for reasons that no one needed to know.

Other writing about illness and the body

Essays

Some years ago around 2006 and 2007, I participated in a website called TheNervousBreakdown.com, which is still going strong and presenting some of the best online writing.

While I wrote about a range of subjects for TheNervousBreakdown.com, naturally my attention turned to the body and to illness. In the body–inspired essays, the meditative and often smart–assed approach both complements and veers from the terrain of the original and new letters in *A Life Less Convenient: Letters to My Ex.*

The content rules at that time for TheNervousBreakdown. com forced me in the best way possible to challenge myself. I experimented with voice and tone as I employed a new format and reached a different audience. In my essays for this site, I grew less tense, less intentionally spartan with language and more concerned with emotional landscapes.

TheNervousBreakdown.com insisted on a stylistic format that was easy on the eyes to aid comprehension for those reading online—hence the one–line or two–line blurbs of text one after the other. I edited my content and style to have impact via these specific layout constraints, which are reproduced in this book with some modifications from the original online publication. Original essays included links that are not included as many are now obsolete. Some phrasing related to links or to other now irrelevant events have also been removed.

My purpose in including these essays is neither to replicate an online user's experience of my writing nor to be true to the original versions. I included two of the health–focused essays as an addendum to the experience expressed through the letters.

The first is titled, "Transcendent Sensation Seeking, or: I Wonder if Cenobites Dream of Being Tied Up with Soft, Silk Scarves." My perspectives on health, mortality and vulnerability have not changed since the original publication. The second is titled, "And I Here I Stand, With Ambivalence, Breast Tenderness, and Tidbit," which documents one of my scares with a breast lump and my first encounter of the squishing kind with a mammogram.

Transcendent sensation seeking or: I wonder if cenobites dream of being tied up with soft, silk scarves

The first time I saw *The Deer Hunter*, I sprawled on the floor of my parents' den on a comforter from my bed, determined to stay up well beyond my usual bedtime. I steeled myself to watch it until the end.

I couldn't articulate the feelings that rocked me after seeing *The Deer Hunter*. Uneasy truths began to articulate themselves, if only through inchoate reactions to certain scenes that wouldn't leave me and still haven't. Movies and books—not trips to church or Catholic schooling or parental lectures—sparked my existential questions about *how to be* and *how things are*.

The movie sparked internal dialogues that centered on the experience of suffering and fear: the inevitable travails of each person's journey, the quietly echoing horror that colors a life gone awry.

Most importantly, I began to think of suffering in relation to the solitude of existing in our own skulls while living in an inherently imperfect, unpredictable world.

My template for processing experience took shape....

"Stanley, see this? This is this. This ain't something else. This is this. From now on, you're on your own."

· · · · · ·

There is plenty that is scary about unending disease.

I say "unending" for a reason: despite the well–intentioned prattling of others, I have not expected a remission, given the severity of the symptoms, the ANA count, the other diagnoses, and the drug cocktail I've needed from the beginning, lest I pitifully howl on the kitchen floor.

I have never had a remission since starting the sickie game in 1998.

I'm thinking menopause might be kind to me and could engender something close to a remission, perhaps the real thing itself, since my lupus and other problems appear to be related to hormonal fluctuations, among other factors.

I've reacted differently to the presence of disease over time.

Once upon a time, I was paranoid about my kidneys.

I suspect my first rheumatologist—the one who diagnosed me—had something to do with that preoccupation.

During my first rheumatology appointment, I learned my diagnosis and received a pamphlet about kidney failure (clearly written for lobotomized patients). The doctor placed another pamphlet in my swollen hand about kidney transplants.

Right there—paranoia.

Paranoia like that leads to hyper–focusing on the body, finding its strengths and indexing its weaknesses.

I worried about what would happen if my kidneys went paws up. Or what if my central nervous system took the brunt of a flare, and by how much, and what would be left?

And what if?

Would I need nursing care twenty–four hours a day? Would I be able to do anything for myself?

I don't know anyone dealing with chronic disease or a severe injury who doesn't have such thoughts now and then take a jog through the brain, leaving muddy footprints that don't wash away.

And life goes on.

But the worry still happens.

And then there are more drugs.

Thanks to a flare in 2003, I have since experienced occassional neuropathies in my hands and feet, sometimes traveling up the limbs but mostly confined to the tips of fingers and toes.

When they first hit with the intensity of a knock–out punch in the sweet spot, I was on my ass. Literally.

I couldn't hold my head up or sit upright for periods of time. A step toward the bathroom brought unbelievable nausea and strikingly bizarre nerve pain. I had no energy as the flare took over.

I waited for this hurricane to pass. I waited to see what would remain for rebuilding.

I did not get my nerves back intact. My life changed.

I had to investigate other medications and to see a neurologist.

There a flare, here a different lifestyle as a direct result.

The fears come in waves. What parts of me will take the hit? What will relationships look like? What will work look like?

Yet I had these thoughts long before surgeries, illnesses, and medications touched my life. Maybe everyone does. Maybe many people don't. But shit, I'm not them.

Maybe I was a truly freakin' weird little kid. We're talking single digits here.

I learned about finality, the lack of second chances with bodily integrity, and the ability to get hurt, to be made un–whole and vulnerable, through a Thanksgiving get–together when I was roughly five or so.

For the final kindergarten class just before the Thanksgiving holiday, the teacher told us to bring an apple and raisins. She said she would give us the rest of the supplies—toothpicks with fancy colored cellophane thingies, glue, scissors and construction paper.

We made turkeys. She helped us to cut turkey legs from orange construction paper and to glue them onto our apples.

We strung raisins on toothpicks and stuck a bunch of them on the ass of the apple to make a feathery dehydrated tail.

I was unreasonably tickled with this apple turkey.

I warned you I was weird.

I brought it to the Thanksgiving get–together at my aunt's home. There were many relatives. I came up to most people's mid–thighs.

There were also plenty of unknown folks, friends of my aunt's family, impossibly large, unknowable grown–ups who smelled like department stores.

I put my apple turkey on the counter and then visited from person to person, babbling.

When I returned to check on my apple turkey, I saw the unthinkable: people had EATEN HIS TAIL RAISINS CLEAN OFF. I pitched a livid fit.

My mom explained that people thought it was some cute way to serve food. I thought it was MY TURKEY.

My aunt had to retrieve raisins and toothpicks to appease me as we rebuilt his tail and put him in a safe place in the refrigerator. I wanted the evildoers' heads. Promptly.

My folks stayed late.

I remember seeing the litter from the party dredged over tables and counter tops: lipsticked wine goblets and crumpled napkins, tiny bits of cheese with crumbs of fancy crackers.

I was tired and ready to go home. The last of the adults were stringing their way out the door, smelling a lot less like department stores.

At some point, I must have fallen asleep. The next thing I knew, I was on my mom's lap, listening to her talk to my aunt before leaving. The first thing I wanted was the apple turkey. My aunt left to grab it.

I said to my mom, "People I love won't be taken from me, will they?"

By this point, I was already perfectly aware of my dad's first brush with cancer, despite my limited understanding at the time. I had "helped" to change his bandages at home when I was around two or thereabouts. He was fiftyish then.

I possessed an inchoate sense of the loss and the danger of that time, of how flesh isn't forever, but something about people gnashing my turkey's raisins got my pinafore in a twist. I don't remember what my mom answered.

I got the turkey back, apparently intact. In time, however, the apple caved in and oozed. The raisins developed a crust I've never seen the likes of since.

I now spend much of my existential pondering focused on how drugs and disease alter the body and how our flesh sacks are an ongoing biochemistry project. I discovered that there was a model for this kind of thinking.

Clive Barker's early version of the Cenobite depicted—for some fans, including me—an entity invested merely in experience, in seeing what flesh and its limits can reveal of the self, and not in making a judgment about pleasure or pain, suffering or indifference.

I have tried to take the Cenobites' approach to pain. I try to believe in sensation–hunting, to believe that this embodiment is saying to me, "I have such sights to show you."

I try to conjure the heart of a Cenobite as the little white gauze patches proliferate over my body in various hospitals.

The goal: experience–seeking and acknowledgment, instead of judgment, about a given sensation.

Yeah, right.

I think I can count the number of times I've done this on one hand. Doesn't stop me from aspiring though.

One of those times is a view from being five years old.

I was walking outside with my uncle and my dad near a farm. The cattle stared back at us from behind an unusual fence. I knew it wasn't like the other fences I saw around the horses.

I asked about it. The adults explained that the fence was "electrified," a word that meant nothing to me.

Their tone of voice, however, signaled something that meant everything to me: it signaled, "Interesting New Frontier You Should Explore No Matter What."

And I did.

I took steps toward the fence, the inevitable already beautifully in progress. One of them grabbed my shoulder and said, "You'll get a shock like you do from the carpet, but worse."

I managed to breakaway from the grasp and edged toward the fence when I heard, "No, no, that'll hurt," which, of course, meant one thing . . .

Touch it.

Find out because curiosity hurts worse than the burns.

And I did.

What I remember is seeing my arms out straight and my hands cartoonishly extended in front of me, a B–movie zombie lumbering toward the fence.

I grabbed it, harshly, and screamed when the jolt hit.

I looked down to find lines from the fence on my palms.

I hollered. I remember that.

Crying meant I knew the consequences. Crying didn't mean I regretted a thing. I didn't.

This is how an electrified fence feels, I thought.

It hurt, and it wasn't something else.

It's *this*.

I was on my own then.

Ambivalence, breast tenderness, and Tidbit

This essay is about as tasteful as bedazzling a pair of acid–washed jeans with pink rhinestones.

This is an essay about boobs.

Specifically, my boobs.

I'm on good terms with the girls, for the most part. Obviously, we go way back. They're there for me.

Our relationship is changing, and that has given me cause for concern.

Overall, I happen to adore them.

I realize the rule is you are allowed to adore your boobs only if you bought them from the right surgeon. Even then, you are allowed to adore them only if they aren't resting on your collarbones or as wall–eyed as an inbred walrus.

As a woman, I often get the feeling that there are plenty of things about my bits that I'm not supposed to adore, like the stretch mark on my right hip that looks like a racing stripe (with the right color for it, no less), or the series of small, round scars high on my belly from tick bites acquired during obsessive midnight walks.

A former boss—the senior lawyer—guessed that my breasts were a B and a half.

As you might imagine, there are many things I could say about that former boss, but won't.

I'll go with his assessment of my size, though I can easily remember being twenty–six years old at eighty–six pounds from a lupus flare: I could poke at the sharp definition of ribs through my nipples.

The twins have changed as I have, which is why their recent behavior concerns me.

I have been in a fairly good place health–wise; in other words, I'm mostly staying at the same sickie level with the same problems in the manageable zone. Imagine the shock from my doctor some months ago when he confirmed the sensation of a seeming "mass" in my right breast.

I was lying on my back on the doctor's table, staring at a new mobile of blue butterflies dancing from the ceiling, as he prodded a lump near my armpit.

"The structure is abnormal," he said.

"Yeah, that's not what I normally feel like, this hardness here," I said, my finger looping over his to make the point.

It'll be fine, I thought, my fingertips still pressing on the lump I named "Tidbit."

It occurred to me suddenly that Tidbit was living rent–free in my body. The bitch.

It'll be fine.

Simultaneously, I thought, "I'm not that gullible, and life isn't that easy."

Of course.

My body has already betrayed me in other ways. Why not this?

My boobs might not be there for me someday. Enough women have loved and lost theirs.

It's like any relationship: as perfect as we may be together, my boobs and me, a weakness might break through us.

Imperfection easily begets betrayal.

My doctor ordered a mammogram, the first in my life, and an ultrasound of Rightie and Tidbit.

I told my father about what had happened.

I told him many thoughts.

I told him my intention to lop off my breast, if possible, at the quickest sign of trouble because I cared more about living than about a nice rack.

I told him that I wasn't one of those women who would fight for my breast, though I would mourn it, and that if the worst were to occur, I didn't see my relationship to my body changing.

He told me the story of J., who was also known as "Pop Pop" to his grandchildren. J. developed severe diabetes that required the amputation of both legs at the knee.

After the surgery, his grandchildren spontaneously took to calling him "Pop Pop Stump Stump," which never ceased to entertain the hell out of J.

When J. was asked about his amputations and the impact on his sense of self, he replied: "I didn't live in those legs. I'm still me."

Then he'd laugh again at his new nickname.

"That's true," I mulled after hearing the story.

I didn't live in my tits.

I'm more than the sum of my boobs, though I love them both dearly.

I'd still go on, with or without Rightie.

· · · · · ·

"And if thine eye causeth thee to stumble, pluck it out, and cast it from thee . . ."

—Matthew 18:9

· · · · · ·

I sat with other women of all ages in one cubby of the waiting room, where we picked at a table of magazines, chafing against our standardized blue togas wrapped tightly against us.

I watched women from the cubby across the aisle pick at their table of magazines and rise as their names were called to go Back There where the squishing machine did its boob business.

When I heard my name, I didn't so much rise as catapult to my feet and speed walk to a short, round woman in blue scrubs that matched my toga.

I could smell something clean and soapy in her shiny bob as she motioned for me to follow her into a room with the squishing machine.

"First I'll need you to sit for some questions. Do you smoke?"

"No, not now."

"Before?"

"Yes, ages nineteen to twenty. Menthols and cloves mostly."

"Do you drink?"

"No."

"Never?"

"Never."

"Okay, now I hate to ask you this question, but it's required."

I bristled. She smiled sweetly and tilted her head.

"Do you have implants?"

I smiled despite myself and stared down at my chest.

"No."

"I was about to say, if you did, you seriously got cheated."

I zeroed in on a few broken capillaries on her cheeks as she asked more questions.

Finally, it was time to stand and face the machine.

"Drop one sleeve down and leave the other on. Now scoot over here."

She gripped my hips and turned my body to the angle needed for the machine.

I tried to picture myself as Athena or Diana in a revealing toga, powerful and regal. I immediately felt pitiful for trying, realizing I was no goddess.

I was an average thirty–something standing half–naked in a suburban hospital and feeling scared shitless of a freeloading mystery named Tidbit.

And I had a strange, insulting woman's hand on my breast.

"I'm sure you've heard horror stories of women's experiences with mammograms."

"Yep."

I spotted more broken capillaries on her nose.

Seriously cheated, eh?

I felt bad for indulging in a pissing contest in my head over size.

Does size really matter after all?

"We'll manage to get you into this machine. You'll fit."

I watched her reshape my breast to fit onto a cold plate.

It looked filleted after a transparent panel lowered onto the plate, flattening Rightie completely.

"Wow, this is really tight."

"It'll be over really soon. Hold your breath."

As I inhaled, I glanced down and was immediately transfixed by how large my breast appeared in its squished state.

I pondered the new shape that was attached to my body. I couldn't stop looking.

"I look so big!" It was out of my mouth before I could stop myself.

"We might have to take that one again."

"Why?"

"Because your head was in the way when you were staring at your breast…Wait, no, I got only the very top of your head. Clear view of the breast. Done."

I couldn't resist: "I'm SO big."

I started laughing. I was being ridiculous. I was supposed to be living in a hotel by Monday night of the following week for work. I was frightened out of my mind.

"I get a lot of shots of the tops of heads because women look down at the sight of their squashed breasts," she laughed.

I decided I would try to like her as she grabbed Leftie for comparison pictures.

· · · · · ·

I learned later from the radiologist who read my pictures that I am "normal."

This is a confusing term.

Then I returned to my doctor's office, reclined on the table, my fingers and his poking at Tidbit.

"It still feels abnormal, but you should be reassured with the results of the pictures."

"I am, but why do I feel different here than I used to be?"

We batted around ideas. There could be something going on in non–breast tissue. It could be ectopic breast tissue. There could be anything.

"We'll continue to monitor it. If needed, we'll send you to a breast surgeon for another opinion, but keep doing self–checks to see if there are further changes."

Life in a nutshell: something may or may not be there; something is off; I might grasp it or not; and it may or may not hurt me.

I come to an uneasy truce, locating peace in ambiguity.

I stare at my right breast in mirrors whenever there's a chance.

Last night, I stretched on my bed, reconnoitered the mystery of Tidbit, and giddily recalled my pictures.

I'm SO big.

Jennifer Clare Burke

Gratitude

A big thank you to Sara Lando, who has graciously allowed me to use her photo for the cover, and to Stephen H. Segal, whose editing made the needed difference in my writing.

From Sara Lando:

Born and raised in Bassano del Grappa, I work among Bassano, Milano and Los Angeles as a portrait photographer and photoretoucher. Among others, I've had the pleasure to work with: De Agostini, Canon, Nokia, Samsung, Ubisoft, Radio Company, Astor Hotel, *Aria*, Manfrotto, Progetto25zero1, *Digital Camera*, *Pig*, Digital Life Style, *Foto Cult*, and *Trip*. Please visit saralando.com.

From Stephen H. Segal:

Stephen H. Segal is a Hugo Award–winning editor, designer, and writer based in Philadelphia, where he is editor in chief of the *Philadelphia Weekly*. His first book, *GEEK WISDOM: The Sacred Teachings of Nerd Culture*, was published in August 2011. Previously, as editorial and creative director of *Weird Tales*, he led the 21st–century revamp of that pioneering magazine of fantastic literature. He is online at stephenhsegal.com.

Resources

Arthritis Foundation
arthritis.org
1330 W. Peachtree Street
Suite 100
Atlanta, GA 30309
Main: (404) 872–7100

Lupus Foundation of America
lupus.org
2000 L Street, N.W., Suite 410
Washington, DC 20036
Main: (202) 349–1155 (8:30 a.m.—5 p.m. ET, Monday—
Friday)
Information request line: (English / Para informacíon en
español) (800)–558–0121

Sjögren's Syndrome Foundation
sjogrens.org
6707 Democracy Boulevard, Suite 325
Bethesda, MD 20817
Toll Free: (800) 475–6473

About Homofactus Press

We publish complex books for complicated people. The mission of Homofactus Press is to publish books that discuss our complicated relationships to our bodies and identities, with all the complexities and contradictions such an endeavor entails.

Thank you for purchasing a Homofactus Press book. Your purchase enables us to keep doing what we love to do: make great writing available to all people. Learn more about us at homofactuspress.com.

If you enjoyed this book, please consider other Homofactus Press titles:

Self-Organizing Men, edited by Jay Sennett

The Marrow's Telling, by Eli Clare

Two Truths and a Lie, by Scott Turner Schofield

Cripple Poetics, by Petra Kuppers and Neil Marcus

Visible: A Femmethology, Volume 1, edited by Jennifer Clare Burke

Visible: A Femmethology, Volume 2, edited by Jennifer Clare Burke

Kicked Out, edited by Sassafras Lowrey with general editor, Jennifer Clare Burke

CPSIA information can be obtained at www.ICGtesting.com
Printed in the USA
BVOW041638200313

315996BV00001B/50/P